GW01081076

Class Rules

MACMILLAN
SHORT
STORIES

Class
Rules

Bill Lucas and Brian Keaney

MACMILLAN

© Bill Lucas and Brian Keaney 1990

All rights reserved. No reproduction, copy or transmission
of this publication may be made without written permission.

No paragraph of this publication may be reproduced, copied
or transmitted save with written permission or in accordance
with the provisions of the Copyright Designs and Patents Act
1988, or under the terms of any licence permitting limited
copying issued by the Copyright Licensing Agency,
33–4 Alfred Place, London WC1E 7DP.

Any person who does any unauthorised act in relation to
this publication may be liable to criminal prosecution and
civil claims for damages.

First published 1990

Published by
MACMILLAN EDUCATION LTD
Houndmills, Basingstoke, Hampshire RG21 2XS
and London
Companies and representatives
throughout the world

Printed in Hong Kong

British Library Cataloguing in Publication Data
Class rules. – (Macmillan short stories)
I. Lucas, Bill   II. Keaney, Brian
823'.01'08 [FS]
ISBN 0–333–48359–6

Contents

Preface

This is a new kind of short-story collection. Instead of the larger number of stories normally included in anthologies, only six have been selected. Instead of 'notes' or 'follow-up material' added on at the end of the book, a variety of spoken and written tasks have been devised to help develop an understanding of each story as it is read. Thus the book falls naturally into six sections, each of which contains:

- a story – each one representing a different cultural perspective;
- non-literary and factual material – for example, newspaper articles and interviews, maps – to help students gain a fuller understanding of the cultural or geographical background;
- photographs;
- literary extracts, to deepen understanding of themes, characters, ideas and styles and to encourage their further exploration.

Throughout the book there is a variety of tasks of different lengths and complexity. These are always integral to the stories and their follow-up work. Suggestions have been made as to the skill areas which might be developed in each task. However, it is anticipated that they will frequently be amended by teachers or used to practise different skill areas.

A number of written assignments follow each story. They are intended to encourage the range of responses appropriate for GCSE English or English Literature coursework. It is assumed that students and teachers will be involved in the drafting of assignments even though lack of space in this book prevents detailed assistance on this being included.

The assignments at the end of the book are particularly suitable for more extended study of the stories in the selection. As with the rest of the material, they are also suitable for independent study outside the classroom.

Getting Sent For

Agnes Owens

Mrs Sharp knocked timidly on the door marked 'Headmistress'.

'Come in,' a cool voice commanded.

She shuffled in, slightly hunched, clutching a black plastic shopping bag and stood waiting for the headmistress to raise her eyes from the notebook she was engrossed in.

'Do sit down,' said the headmistress when Mrs Sharp coughed apologetically.

Mrs Sharp collapsed into a chair and placed her bag between her feet. The headmistress relinquished the notebook with a sigh and began.

'I'm sorry to bring you here, but recently George has become quite uncontrollable in class. Something will have to be done.'

Mrs Sharp shifted about in the chair and assumed a placating smile.

'Oh dear – I thought he was doing fine. I didn't know –'

'It's been six months since I spoke to you,' interrupted the headmistress, 'and I'm sorry to say he has not improved one bit. In fact he's getting steadily worse.'

Mrs Sharp met the impact of the gold-framed spectacles nervously as she said, 'It's not as if he gets away with anything at home. His Da and me are always on at him, but he pays no attention.'

The headmistress's mouth tightened. 'He will just have to pay attention.'

'What's he done this time?' Mrs Sharp asked with a surly edge to her voice.

'He runs in and out of class when the teacher's back is turned and distracts the other children.'

Mrs Sharp eased out her breath. 'Is that all?'

The headmistress was incredulous. 'Is that all? With twenty-five pupils in a class, one disruptive element can ruin everything. It's difficult enough to push things into their heads as it is –' She broke off.

'Seems to me they're easily distracted,' said Mrs Sharp.

'Well children are, you know.' The headmistress allowed a frosty smile to crease her lips.

'Maybe he's not the only one who runs about,' observed Mrs Sharp mildly.

'Mrs Sharp, I assure you George is the main trouble-maker,

1

otherwise I would not have sent for you.'

The light from the headmistress's spectacles was as blinding as a torch.

Mrs Sharp shrank back. 'I'm not meaning to be cheeky, but George isn't a bad boy. I can hardly credit he's the worst in the class.'

The headmistress conceded, 'No, I wouldn't say he's the worst. There are some pupils I've washed my hands of. As yet there's still hope for George. That's why I sent for you. If he puts his mind to it he can work quite well, but let's face it, if he's going to continue the way he's doing, he'll end up in a harsher place than this school.'

Mrs Sharp beamed as if she was hearing fulsome praise. 'You mean he's clever?'

'I wouldn't say he's clever,' said the headmistress cautiously, 'but he's got potential. But really,' she snapped, 'it's more his behaviour than this potential that worries us.'

Mrs Sharp tugged her wispy hair dreamily. 'I always knew George had it in him. He was such a bright baby. Do you know he opened his eyes and stared straight at me when he was a day old. Sharp by name, and sharp by nature – that's what his Da always said.'

'That may be,' said the headmistress, taking off her spectacles and rubbing her eyes, 'but sharp is not what I'm looking for.'

Then, aware of Mrs Sharp's intent inspection of her naked face, she quickly replaced them, adding, 'Another thing. He never does any homework.'

'I never knew he had any,' said Mrs Sharp, surprised. 'Mind you we've often asked him "Don't you get any homework?" and straight away he answers "We don't get any" –'

The headmistress broke in. 'He's an incorrigible liar.'

'Liar?' Mrs Sharp clutched the collar of her bottle-green coat.

'Last week he was late for school. He said it was because you made him stay and tidy his room.'

Mrs Sharp's eyes flickered. 'What day was that?'

'Last Tuesday.' The headmistress leaned over the desk. 'Did you?'

'I don't know what made him say that,' said Mrs Sharp in wonderment.

'Because he's an incorrigible liar.'

Mrs Sharp strove to be reasonable. 'Most kids tell lies now and again to get out of a spot of bother.'

'George tells more lies than most – mind you,' the headmistresses's lips twisted with humour, 'we were all amused at the idea of George tidying, considering he's the untidiest boy in the class.'

Mrs Sharp reared up. 'Oh, is he? Well let me tell you he's tidy when he leaves the house. I make him wash his face and comb his hair every day. How the devil should I know what he gets up to when he leaves?'

'Keep calm, Mrs Sharp. I'm sure you do your best under the circumstances.'

'What circumstances?'

'Don't you work?' the headmistress asked pleasantly.

Mrs Sharp sagged. She had a presentiment of doom. Her husband had never liked her working. 'A woman's place is in the home,' he always said when any crisis arose – despite the fact that her income was a necessity.

'Yes,' she said.

'Of course,' said the headmistress, her spectacles directed towards the top of Mrs Sharp's head, 'I understand that many mothers work nowadays, but unfortunately they are producing a generation of latch-key children running wild. Far be it for me to judge the parents' circumstances, but I think a child's welfare comes first.' She smiled toothily. 'Perhaps I'm old-fashioned, but –'

'I suppose you're going to tell me a woman's place is in the home?' asked Mrs Sharp, through tight lips.

'If she has children, I would say so.'

Mrs Sharp threw caution to the wind. 'If I didn't work George wouldn't have any uniform to go to school with –'

She broke off at the entrance of an agitated tangle-haired young woman.

'I'm sorry Miss McHare,' said the young woman, 'I didn't know you were with someone –'

'That's all right,' said the headmistress. 'What is it?'

'It's George Sharp again.'

'Dear, dear!' The headmistress braced herself while Mrs Sharp slumped.

'He was fighting, in the playground. Ken Wilson has a whopper of an eye. Sharp is outside. I was going to send him in, but if you're engaged –'

The headmistress addressed Mrs Sharp. 'You see what I mean. It just had to be George again.'

She turned to the young teacher. 'This is George's mother.'

'Good morning,' said the young teacher, without enthusiasm.

'How do you know George started it?' asked Mrs Sharp, thrusting her pale face upwards. The headmistress stiffened. She stood up and towered above Mrs Sharp like a female Gulliver. Mrs Sharp pointed her chin at a right angle in an effort to focus properly.

The headmistress ordered, 'Bring the boy in.'

George Sharp shuffled in, tall and gangling, in contrast to his hunched mother, who gave him a weak smile when he looked at her blankly.

'Now,' said the headmistress, 'I hear you've been fighting.'

George nodded.

'You know fighting is forbidden within these grounds.'

'Ken Wilson was fighting as well,' he replied hoarsely, squinting through strands of dank hair.

'Ken Wilson is a delicate boy who does not fight.'

'He kicked me,' George mumbled, his eyes swivelling down to his sandshoes.

The headmistress explained to no one in particular, 'Of course George is not above telling lies.'

Mrs Sharp rose from her chair like a startled bird. 'Listen son, did that boy kick you?'

'Yes Ma,' George said eagerly.

'Where?'

He pointed vaguely to his leg.

'Pull up your trouser.'

George did so.

'Look,' said Mrs Sharp triumphantly, 'that's a black and blue mark.'

'Looks more like dirt,' tittered the young teacher.

'Dirt is it?' Mrs Sharp rubbed the mark. George winced.

'That's sore.'

'It's a kick mark. Deny it if you can.'

'Come now,' said the headmistress, 'we're not in a courtroom. Besides, whether it's a kick mark or not doesn't prove a thing. Possibly it was done in retaliation. Frankly I don't see Ken Wilson starting it. He hasn't got the stamina.'

'Is that so?' said Mrs Sharp. 'I know Ken Wilson better than you, and he's no better than any other kid when it comes to starting fights. He's well known for throwing stones and kicking cats –'

The headmistress intervened. 'In any case this is beside the point. I brought you here to discuss George's behaviour in general, and not this matter in particular.'

'And bloody well wasted my time,' retorted Mrs Sharp.

The headmistress's mouth fell open at the effrontery. She turned to the young teacher.

'You may go now, Miss Tilly,' adding ominously to George, 'You too, Sharp, I'll deal with you later.'

George gave his mother an anguished look as he was led out.

'Don't worry,' she called to him.

The headmistress said, 'I don't know what you mean by that, because I think your son has plenty to worry about.'

Mrs Sharp stood up placing her hands on her hips. Her cheeks were now flushed.

'You know what I think – I think this is a case of persecution. I mean the way you carried on about George fighting just proves it. And all this guff about him distracting the class – well if that flibbery gibbery miss is an example of a teacher then no wonder the class is easily distracted. Furthermore,' she continued wildly before the headmistress could draw her breath, 'I'll be writing to the authorities to let them know how my son is treated. Don't think they won't be interested because all this bullying in school is getting a big write-up nowadays.'

'How dare you talk to me like that,' said the headmistress, visibly white round the nose. 'It's your son who is the bully.'

Mrs Sharp jeered, 'So now he's a bully. While you're at it is there anything else? I suppose if you had your way he'd be off to a remand home.'

'No doubt he'll get there of his own accord.'

The remark was lost on Mrs Sharp, now launched into a tirade of reprisal for all injustices perpetrated against working-class children and her George in particular. The headmistress froze in the face of such eloquence, which was eventually summed up by the final denunciation:

'So if I was you I'd hand in my notice before all this happens. Anyway you're too old for the job. It stands to reason your nerves are all shook up. It's a well-known fact that spinster teachers usually end cracking up and being carted off.'

The change in their complexions was remarkable. The headmistress was flushed purple with rage and Mrs Sharp was pallid with conviction.

There was a space of silence. Then the headmistress managed to say, 'Get out – before I call the janitor.'

Mrs Sharp gave a hard laugh. 'Threats is it now? Still I'm not bothered, for it seems to me you've got all the signs of cracking up right now. By the way if you lay one finger on George I'll put you on a charge.'

She flounced out of the room when the headmistress picked up the telephone, and banged the door behind her. The headmistress replaced the receiver without dialling, then sat down at the desk with her head in her hands, staring at the open notebook.

Outside Mrs Sharp joined a woman waiting against the school

railings, eating crisps.

'How did you get on?' the woman asked.

Mrs Sharp rummaged in her plastic bag and brought out a packet of cigarettes. Before she shoved one into her mouth she said, 'Tried to put me in my place she did – well I soon showed her she wasn't dealing with some kind of underling –'

The woman threw the empty crisp packet on to the grass.

'What about George?'

Mrs Sharp looked bitter. 'See that boy – he's a proper devil. Wait till I get him home and I'll beat the daylights out of him. I'll teach him to get me sent for.'

Working mothers

'I understand that many mothers work nowadays, but unfortunately they are producing a generation of latch-key children running wild.'

Read

The mother in this story is made to feel responsible for her son's behaviour by the headmistress. Read this article which explores the issue from a working mother's point of view.

Unsympathetic teachers can make the working mother's life a misery. Are their criticisms fair? asks Edwina Conner

'Couldn't you wait a year before taking up the job?' That was the somewhat frosty response from my small daughter's headmistress when I told her that I'd accepted a post with a local book publishing company while Anna was still in her very first term at school.

How mean, I thought. I'd been waiting for an opportunity like this ever since I struggled to put on Anna's first nappy five years before. Didn't this woman know that when you are handicapped with what the male executive considers to be multiple disadvantages in a female – lacking recent experience, being married, possessing a child – you can't just say, 'thanks *awfully* for giving me the job. I'd love it *next year*'?

Seeing my face fall, she went on: 'She's so little, she doesn't understand about work, she likes to know you're at home. She'll feel insecure if she thinks you're not there and she doesn't know where you are.'

I agreed with all that, but had already decided that these were problems I could overcome by explaining my feelings to Anna, having a word with my employer, taking on a kind and reliable au pair and generally making the transition from housebound mother to frantic working mother slowly.

Guilt sets in

The trouble was that this headmistress had confirmed my feelings of guilt about working – feelings that are rarely far from the surface for any mother with a job outside the home. I wanted her reassurance, not disapproval. Why? Probably because I'm the product of a generation that doesn't question authority in the way children do today. Teachers still frighten me. What they say matters a lot; their words have the ring of truth, whereas my own beliefs seem altogether less reliable.

That was five years ago – Anna has now moved on – and attitudes at the school have changed. The new headmistress sports a *Supergran* badge on her lapel. She and her staff – mostly working mothers themselves – are sympathetic to the problems and do not feel children suffer just because their mothers work. One says: 'The only difference I notice is that these children tend to be a bit spoilt – partly because their mothers try and compensate for not being at home so much, partly because the parents are earning more money and can afford to buy them more treats.'

 ... there is no evidence to show children suffer just because their mothers work ... according to a study by the US National Academy of Science ...

All the teachers at this school (whether or not they are mothers themselves), appear to go out of their way to help women with problems. As another says: 'If a mother comes to me and says, "Look, I've got a job, can I please drop my child off 10 or 15 minutes early in the morning, or pick him up a bit late" that's fine . . . I'm always here anyway, preparing for the day or clearing up.'

On the other hand, they also feel that a great many women simply do not make satisfactory arrangements for their children after school. The reception class teacher says: 'Sometimes we're left with a child until 4.30 and we literally don't know what to do with him. There's no answer when we telephone home and he doesn't know who's picking him up. It's horrible for the child and a great worry for the school. If a different person comes to collect him every day he gets confused. A young child can't possibly be expected to remember whether he's supposed to be going home with Johnny, or Mary, or whoever. During the day he'll start worrying about it, and then he'll lose concentration. His work will suffer, so will his behaviour, so will I! But,' she adds, 'it's not necessarily the working mothers who neglect their children. There are several women who don't work, have all the time in the world and still don't get their act together.'

This anxiety about unsatisfactory care arrangements is echoed by the headmaster of a progressive junior school in East Sussex. While he feels that it is a teacher's duty to give all parents support, and to help working mothers wherever possible, he does worry about the harm that might come to children who have to make their own way home.

'We have two little girls here of seven and eight who have to walk through a housing estate, down the high street and then catch a bus home, all on their own. I know their mother can't come and get them, but I don't like it. So I telephoned the bus company and asked if they would get the conductor to keep an eye on them. Many parents simply aren't aware that they could be neglecting their children.'

This headmaster thinks that responsible women who are aware of the danger of neglect probably have little to worry about; they're the ones who bend over backwards to compensate. But some teachers make them feel guilty because of their own inadequacies. Some teachers – particularly those who are unmarried – have had very little experience of life outside an educational establishment. They go to school, attend college, come back to school. What do they know about the problems of working mothers? Others, usually older women who stayed at home for a long time with their children, simply envy the freedom women have today.

GOOD HOUSEKEEPING **APRIL 1986**

Talk

In groups discuss your reactions to these statements:

● Mothers should not work while their children are at school.
● Mothers should feel free to work once their children have settled into Primary school.
● Mothers have no reason to feel guilty about working.
● A woman's place is in the home.
● Schools should make more effort to understand the needs of working mothers.
● More fathers should give up work to look after their children.
● It is always the mother who has to take time off work to look after the children.

In groups:

● Make a list of all the reasons why women work that you can think of. Are they the same as the reasons why men work?
● List the practical problems which face working mothers.
● Discuss the measures that schools could take to support mothers like Mrs Sharp.

Assignment

A day in the life of Mrs Sharp.

Stage 1   Decide who else you think would have made up the Sharp family apart from George and his mother. Make brief notes on each member of the family; age, character etc.

Stage 2   List the main things that you think Mrs Sharp would do in a day.

Stage 3   Make sure you have a clear idea of what happened to Mrs Sharp on the day described in the story. This will involve imagining what happened before she went to school and the events of later that day.

Write about a day in her life which includes the events of *'Getting Sent For'*.

A war of words

'Anyway you're getting too old for the job.'
'I'm sure you do your best under the circumstances.'

Talk

In groups:

● Look at these words which were taken from the story. Agree where each one is used. Look up the meanings of any you do not understand.

timidly	snapped	shifted
jeered	placating	froze
nervously	apologetically	conceded
beamed	shuffled	flounced
surly	incredulous	shrank back
staring	commanded	flushed.

● Decide which of them apply to the headmistress, which to Mrs Sharp. Make two lists.
● Which words suggest that the person they are describing is confident and in control of the situation.

Which of the two central women is more confident of her power at the start of the story? Explain your reasons. Describe how things have changed by the end of the story.

Turning-points

'It's a well-known fact that spinster teachers usually end cracking up and being carted off.'

Mrs Sharp's attack on the headmistress produces a sudden change in the relationship between them and is one clear turning-point in the story.

Talk

In groups, choose two other important moments in the story. Explain your choices.

In pairs, read aloud the dialogue involving Mrs Sharp and the headmistress. Decide which of the lines have the most effect as you read them. Choose the three most powerful lines.

Role play

In pairs, act out the interview. Include the three most powerful lines you have just selected, but *make up* the rest of the scene from what you can remember of it.

In pairs, act out the scene as you think it would have been if:

● Mrs Sharp had been a wealthy woman who had chosen not to work;
● the headmistress had been a headmaster.

Assignment

Either   Write out your alternative interviews as two scripts.

Or   'I'll be writing to the authorities to let them know how my son is treated.'

Imagine you are Mrs Sharp. Write a letter of complaint to her local education authority.

Stage 1   Work out what George is being accused of and what you think actually happened at school.

Stage 2   Decide how you would want to present the interview with the headmistress and what she said to you about George six months ago.

Stage 3   Choose a style of writing that you think Mrs Sharp would be most likely to use.

Disruption in class

'With twenty-five pupils in a class, one disruptive element can ruin everything.'

There have been a few disruptive students in school since schooling began. Occasionally, students have taken to the streets. Recently there has been a major report on violence in schools.

Read

Study this article based on some of the evidence used by the Elton Committee. Read the poem which follows it and look at the photographs.

> But are "violence and indiscipline" really so serious – and worsening? While disruptive behaviour certainly makes teachers' lives difficult, there is little independent evidence that it is anywhere near as bad as the reports suggest, or getting worse on so dramatic a scale. Figures issued by teaching unions are often based on a tiny and unrepresentative sample – a fact which has prompted the Elton Committee to conduct a fresh survey of its own.
>
> Most teachers take a cautious view. Few can recall more than one or two incidents of pupils actually hitting teachers at any time in their career and it was usually a colleague. But they take assaults very seriously.

Aggressive behaviour, they admit, is more common than before – but most likely to occur between children in the playground and not during class. Genuinely disruptive children, whose naughtiness, tantrums, and refusal to co-operate upset teaching processes, constitute – as they have always done – the intransigent five per cent, a handful of educational terrorists in every school.

What actually upsets teachers most, according to one educational psychologist, is the "routine disrespect in children's language, swearing and answering back" which is now commonplace – but that is a long way from being confronted with a generation of unteachable kids.

It is hard for teachers to take a dispassionate veiw. As one teacher of ten years' experience put it: "For us, it's like being stuck in the trenches and being asked by someone how the war is going. You just can't tell."

Other experienced teachers are more certain. "There is less violence towards staff than there was," said the head teacher of one inner-city school. "There may be more passive abuse but the level of physical violence towards staff has not increased at all. On the other hand, kids nowadays are much more likely to be aggressive and violent towards each other."

Another teacher said: "We're an inner city school where you would expect fairly severe problems. I've only taught here six years, but I would not say that violence is getting worse. What's changing is society outside school, what people conceive of as violent behaviour, and tolerance levels of both teachers and pupils."

The real problem is not that classrooms are significantly more violent, but that teachers, politicians and the public cannot agree what to do about a gradually evolving problem. Between local education authorities, and even between schools in the same area, approaches to discipline vary. Much depends on the leadership of the head teacher, the loyalty of staff, the kind of training teachers are given, the rate of turnover in the staff room, the quality of links with parents, or even the way the school is laid out.

MICHAEL GRAHAM
THE GUARDIAN, DECEMBER 20, 1986

Disruptive Minority

Rude words on the blackboard,
Crushed chalk on the floor,
Books bunged out the window,
Run out, slam the door.

Teacher's depression
Me and my class
Football in the playground
Connects with school glass.

Cigarettes in the toilet
And nudie books too.
When I leave this dump
Then what will I do?

I'm nothing special,
The school taught me that.
I haven't got brains
And my prospects are flat.

Can't hit back at the system
It's blank, has no features,
So while I'm at school
I'll take it out on the teachers.

ALAN GILBEY

Talk

In groups:
Talk about any disruptive behaviour which you have witnessed in the last year. Describe one incident in detail. What do you think causes such behaviour?

What can schools do about violence? Make a list of all the features of a school which help to produce a calm, disciplined atmosphere.

How important do you think the teacher is in preventing violent behaviour? What qualities would your ideal teacher have? List them.

Parents, teachers and discipline

'Wait till I get him home and I'll beat the daylights out of him.'

Read

Since schools began, parents have sometimes disagreed with the way their children have been treated. Read these three descriptions of schooldays in the early part of this century.

Well, we 'ad one [teacher] an' he was a big pig, a sadistic pig. He delighted in rapping kids' knuckles if you weren't paying attention, daydreaming instead of writing. [Respondent bangs on the table.] 'Wake up, boy! Wake up, boy!' Anyway, one of my pals there, name was Been, he 'ad a younger brother, Arnold, in a lower class. And a kid rushed into our class an' said, 'Eh, Tommy Burrows i'n't 'alf 'itting your Arnold, Wilf.' So Wilf Been and Wilf Williams and me got out of our seats an' rushed into Tommy Burrows's class, and he was doing little Arnold. And we jumped on him and we had 'n down an' we was going, 'We'll have you! Leave our Arnold alone.' In the meantime someone had rushed round the next street, Walter Street, an' my mother was doing 'er washing. She was a tiny woman. She always wore my father's cap and a sack apron. She rolled 'er sleeves up, round the school, into the classroom, 'I'll kill you if you hit my son.' He'd hit both of us, marked us, wealed us, marked all our legs with the stick. We could 'ave sued the 'Education'. She sparred up to him. He was about five ten, six foot. [He] got behind the desk, out the way – he was ever so brave. And they kept us away from school for four days, both of us, because we were marked. It made me the worst boy in the class for hitting the teacher.

The mothers used to come up an' play merry 'ell with the teachers for caning us. Another thing mothers'd go mad about was when we weren't allowed to go to the toilet an' we ended up wetting ourselves. Our Aunt Sally'd be up there all the time, 'cos she was poor but she never used to lay a finger on 'er girls, never. Once she came up and pulled 'er [the teacher's] hairpins out. Then she caught hold of 'er hair an' started to drag 'er out of the classroom and into the playground. Of course, we kids was enjoying every minute of it, shouting an' cheering, 'Go on, 'ave 'er!' And the kids in the other classes saw what was happening, an' they pushed their teachers aside an' ran out to join us. It was a proper riot. We was all shouting and screaming. Anyway, they got us back in eventually, an' Aunt Sally got summonsed, fined five pounds for that.

Schoolchildren marching through London

One day my sister got to school late and this German governess hit her. She fell on the pipes and had to have three stitches in her lip. Of course, the kids went home and told my dad. My dad went up there and he lopped her one. My dad had seven days' imprisonment for it. She had it out on me after when I used to go to school. Hit me across the legs with a cane and all like that. So anyway, we moved away from there and we went to Moorfields. And lo and behold, who do you think we've got for a governess? This bloody old governess. And I thought, no. I goes home to my dad. I said, 'Dad, who do you think we've got for a governess?' He said, 'I don't know'. I said, 'Miss Davey.' He said, 'Now, don't you say anything to her. Take no notice of her. Don't do anything. So anyway, the woman next door has got a boy going to the same school. This governess picks this little boy out. Of course, this woman drinks a lot. She goes up to the school; she hits her; she makes her blind. She got fined twenty pounds for assault. All the women made a collection, then went and fetched her out of prison with rosettes and white hats on. One morning it was snowing and it was ever so cold. And she hit one little kid right across the legs. So we couldn't stick that. So I say to all the kids, 'Come on, let's have a go at her.' And we did. We snowballed her and all. And she had a wig. We ripped her wig off, rubbed her head in ice balls and threw her into this big bin and we shut the door up. And, of course, the school head, or whoever it was, comes down and he says, 'What's going on here?' I said, 'She's been so cruel to us all that we chucked her in the bin.'

STEPHEN HUMPHRIES *HOOLIGANS OR REBELS?*

Talk

- What do these memories have in common with the situation described in the story?
- How do you think George's behaviour at school was influenced by his mother's treatment of him at home?
- 'How do you know George started it?'
  What evidence is there in this story that George might have been unfairly treated?
- Who deserves most sympathy in the story – Mrs Sharp, George Sharp, Miss McHare, or the young teacher Miss Tilly?
- How do you think George Sharp should have been treated by
  a) his school?
  b) his mother?

Assignment

Either Write a story involving a disruptive student, one or both parents and a teacher. Use the story to explore some of the issues which have been highlighted by the material you have studied.

Or 'Don't think they won't be interested because all this bullying in school is getting a big write-up nowadays.'
Write a feature on bullying in schools for your local newspaper. Explore some of the issues behind violent behaviour and suggest what schools should be doing to prevent this.

Prize Giving

Moy McCrory

They were proud anxious parents. She, nervous and fidgety in a
grey coat. He, inarticulate, choking on pride. Their pride was the
one thing that was holding them together, tying up the nerve ends
with a certainty, for they were sure of their daughter. Their anxieties
were for themselves.

She looked down at herself. Her bust was too big and her back
too narrow. The shoulder seams of her coat drooped too much
around the arms, loose and ungainly while the buttons strained over
her chest. She did not fit into her clothes. The lines of her body
were not well tailored. There was always something too big or too
small or too long. She wore a large diamante brooch over her left
breast and wondered if it was a mistake. The more she thought
about it, the more awkward it looked, pinned on, the size of a
dinner plate. It caught her eye unashamedly like a crude trophy,
drawing attention to her. She did not want attention, especially
there! She was not proud of herself, she would have preferred to
sink out of sight. Her hand reached up and quickly unpinned the
clasp. She shut it and stowed it carefully in her pocket. After that
she felt safer and the feeling of pride for Siobhan engulfed her
again. She and her husband rose on peaks only to crash from
pleasure to nervousness, pride to terror.

He was unable to speak. He was scared that the words would
come out backwards when he tried to talk or he would say the
wrong thing. Sentences always went askew in his mouth. As long as
he had been in England words were his master, calling the tune to
the graceless dancer. Sometimes when he heard himself talking his
voice sounded so hesitant, so unsure, that it was bitter for him to try
to listen. He had been good at school (his wife agreed that Siobhan
took after him), he had been confident and knew the right answers;
but that was a long time ago. He lost his nerve. Now, when he was
worried about using the wrong word or tense, he would leave them
out altogether rather than make a mistake. Tonight he was dumb
with fear.

She linked her husband's arm to hold herself up. She could not
let Siobhan down tonight. All the way to the hall she was scared of
falling over with her weak ankle and wished that she had not worn
the shoes with those stupid heels to make her taller, for they made
her legs look so much thinner. She felt all unbalanced; heavy and
solid on top, tapering to a point where her feet should have been.

She looked down at the wasted muscles in her calves and the
delicate floriate vein that had first blossomed when she was
pregnant and had stayed, faded now into a finely drawn root. If she
let go of his arm she would go down like a bowling skittle. She
hoped that she would not get mud all over her stockings.

'Don't walk so fast,' she pleaded.

'Fast!' he thought ironically. When he owed it to his child to be a
youthful playing parent he got breathless with his weak heart and
had to gasp apologies. Walks together were torture, Siobhan
wanted to run everywhere or to skip. And now his wife was asking
him to slow down.

'We'll be late, we'll miss the start,' he said and he tightened his
grip on her arm to support her and pull her along.

To arrive late meant that all heads would turn to watch, giving
them disapproving glances as they shuffled looking for their seats.
He could already hear their errant footsteps echo in the sepulchral
chamber of the hall. Disgraceful. Like turning up drunk to a funeral.
He would do anything to avoid eyes on him; creep in in the dark if
he could, quietly, softly, to disappear, extinguished by the house
lights. *Nosferatu* of the stalls.

Neither of them could bear up to inspection. They were too old to
be Siobhan's parents. This bright shining child had been a blessing
too late in their lives. The gap in age seemed to widen, not close,
as Siobhan grew older and sometimes they thought that they could
see envy in her for the youthful families her friends belonged to,
while her own parents aged visibly. In a metal box under their bed
she kept worn brown photographs of young men and women in full
bloom, lost generations of family, the blue grey death certificates in
a tight wedge, musty with the smell of damp, stale when the lid was
lifted. Their marriage certificate lay folded neatly. Their birth
certificates were all together. His, faded and torn, the writing barely
legible as the ink had worn to the dullest grey. The Irish harp still
stood out nobly on a green ground. Here was the pink and yellowed
certificate cracking like dry skin.

PLACE OF BIRTH. . . . .Liverpool

FATHER'S OCCUPATION. . . . .Carter

MOTHER'S SIGNATURE. . .An X

ADDRESS. . . . . . . .Clancy's Boarding House, Hunter Street.

She was English by an accident. They skitted her about it back in
Mayo – because she was so pale.

''Twas the English air,' her mother always said.

The date on her birth certificate seemed to grow larger, more
entrenched with age.

'Surely that can't be right,' she had thought, genuinely shocked, the last time she had looked at it before stowing it away, back out of sight but not mind, into the darkness of the cold box. That was where they both belonged, somewhere out of sight where they would not be an embarrassment to their daughter.

They sat in at night; Siobhan doing homework, always reading, always studying. In the corner the television showed them pictures of ideal families selling toothpaste and cornflakes, laughing with perfect teeth. They became comfortable in their seclusion.

They used to go out. When they were courting they went dancing. Saturday nights were spent at the Grafton Ballroom covered in moving flecks of light from the crystal ball and the feel of the smooth waxed floor underfoot. She remembered the smell of brilliantine on the neatly combed hair of her partners as she stepped out with them to take the floor. She had been a fine careful dancer in those days, but he had the two left feet of a ploughboy and only danced on sufferance. She enrolled him for a course of lessons at Billy Martin's school of dancing but he said he felt embarrassed walking round a room counting 'one two three turn, one two three turn,' and everyone going in different directions. When she married him the dancing stopped. They had few excursions out together. He was not a drinker and although she would not have liked him to go off on his own and come in late smelling of beer and urine like her own father used to, she would nonetheless have enjoyed an occasional trip to the pub. But the more they hid themselves the more difficult it was to break their habits.

When they arrived at the hall there were already groups of people standing around outside in loose gatherings, talking comfortably together, recognising old acquaintances. Glossy, poised and perfect toothed. He felt her hold his hand as the courage drained out of him. Were they the only couple who did not know anybody?

The doors of the foyer were wide open to the street on such a fine summer's evening. His vision swam in the yellow light travelling from the sleeping docks out across the waterfront. It spread over the city bathing everything from the warehouses to the neat new council flats, mushrooming around the industrial estate, in a golden gleam of prosperity. At the Pier Head night-workers waited for the factory buses to take them out for their shifts, while in the distance, but never too far away, the dark slump was baying as it steadily advanced.

At the top of Brownlow Hill the cranes stood out against the skyline. The foundations for the new cathedral had been laid and the first stage of building was over. The crypt was finished, white walled and modern.

'We talk with an accent exceedingly rare,
Meet under a statue exceedingly bare,
And if you want a cathedral
We've got TWO to spare,
In my Liverpool home.'

The audacity of the people, changing the words of the song before it was even finished! He wondered if he would see it in his day. The Anglican cathedral was still not complete after all that time. Cathedrals would not be rushed. At least the Anglicans had built theirs to look like a church, somewhere to go and pray in. The plans for theirs made it look like a space rocket. It would be like going to mass at a launching site. The Orange Lodge were going to have a bloody field day, he thought.

'Well, serves us right.'

He ached trying to move with the times, but how could he when it all got so fast like an uphill rush? His ecumenism was the sort that would live and let live as long as he was not expected to change. He did not mind the idea of Siobhan playing mixed games with a C of E school as long as she was safely back on the school bus to her own Catholic classroom at the end of it.

He felt he had lived all his life by divisions. His own country was divided. The boundary around the North may have just been a red line drawn on maps, but it made it into a different world. The people like goldfish that swelled or shrank according to their habitat, had become diverse. There was something about the set of the eyes of the Ulster Irish, a world-weary thing. His mother used to tell the old story of how Fintan from the seat of Tara had allocated all things to the separate provinces when Ireland was divided up. To the North was bequeathed conflicts and assaults, so that Ulster should be ever battle-scarred and torn. He knew it was just a matter of time before it would all flare up again like the rising in the South. Now he lived in a divided city, torn by religion, its peoples needing two football teams for their different loyalties. It annoyed him when he saw the message on the wall changed to read 'God bless our Popeye'. It hurt him to see how little respect there was between them. The white walled monument rising from the rubble where the workhouse had once stood was important to him.

'This is the first time,' he told Siobhan, 'that two Cathedrals will face each other, recognising the other's existence and bowing with dignity.' Deep down he feared that theirs would not look half as dignified.

Every year the school hired the Philharmonic Hall in the city centre
for prize giving. It was a prestigious affair aimed at attracting new
pupils and satisfying the governors. A local dignitary, a chaplain
who had found fame on the missions, or someone else of note, was
often cajoled into giving a speech. Sometimes a past pupil who had
done well was invited back to present the prizes and the audience
was always swelled by the Old Girls Commission which made a
point of turning up every year. It was one of the better girls' schools
in Liverpool. Generations of schoolgirls passed down through
families from mother to daughter, instilling a sense of loyalty to the
establishment. Moist eyes always greeted the school song, the
gracious Alma Mater.

The choir rehearsed all year for its annual exposure and the band
was keyed into shape. Uniforms had to be pressed and cleaned
ready for the night and the costumiers in Bold Street worked
overtime getting the colours sewn into black robes and unpacking
mortar boards in time to let the smell of camphor fade.

She had starched Siobhan's blouse and ironed it and steamed
the box pleats in the gymslip between brown paper. She hated that
gymslip. As soon as the skirt was sat on the pleats went out of
shape. It was such an impractical uniform she thought, and there
was so much of it too! She had been horrified when the euphoria of
Siobhan's scholarship had worn off and she reckoned what it was
worth in hard cash. There was a uniform grant, but he would not let
her apply for it and risk shaming themselves.

The inventory of uniform still haunted her. It was so long and
there were so many different items. She thought that there were
enough clothes to last a lifetime.

WINTER UNIFORM
4 cream shirts
1 brown and yellow tie
1 brown gymslip
2 cardigans with yellow piping
A greatcoat
A brown tailored mackintosh
1 brown corduroy jockey cap
1 brown and yellow scarf
1 pair of brown gloves
2 pairs of thick brown woollen tights
fawn hose
brown lace-up outdoor shoes
brown leather indoor shoes (slipperette variety)

SUMMER UNIFORM
3 yellow cotton dresses
2 belts
1 brown blazer
1 straw boater with brown trim
3 pairs of white kid gloves
light summer shoes (fawn or brown, no heels)
white ankle socks or nylons

GAMES UNIFORM
1 pair divided skirts
2 airtex shirts
2 pairs white towelling socks
1 pair of white plimsolls
1 pair of track shoes
tennis whites/skirt & blouse or fitted dress

The worst part about it was that everything had to be ordered
from the gents' tailors in town. There was no way anything cheaper
could be substituted. Even the blouses had to be a special off-white
creamy colour that was difficult to copy. A white shirt from a
department store at a fraction of the price would have made
Siobhan stand out, gleaming in her cheap shirt. The list
recommended four as a minimum. She had bought two and washed
one every night. The games uniform seemed totally unnecessary to
her. Why did it require such a special outfit just to play hockey in
and chase balls around a field? Siobhan had to have long divided
skirts with inverted pleats that had to be sent to the dry cleaners
every fortnight. A tennis racquet and a case, a briefcase, a good
fountain pen, a geometry set, mapping pens and a ruler, coloured
pencils, two and a half yards of cotton material for needlework, a
sewing case . . .
They had thought that it would never end.
And the demands from the school never did. It was always the
same. Give generously, give something. Gifts to be raffled, objects
for the sale of work, food for the Christmas hamper, cakes for the
cake stall. One event would no sooner be over than another took its
place and whether it was money for the missions or the school trip
to Chester she had ceased to notice. She knew that there would be
no end to it. It was the same at church. The collection boxes full of
copper and the parish priest angry.

Inside the hall girls were already filling up the stage. They came pouring out of concealed entrances in a flood of brown and yellow school colours to take up their positions on the seating arrangement that curved in a huge semi-circle as far as the eye could see.

The stage was tiered, with a flat area usually kept for the concert pianist or soloist. Visiting orchestras played there and massed choirs of Welshmen. Brass band ensembles in spotless military uniforms that they hung in polythene bags inside the coach as soon as they had finished, even the odd rock concert had graced the boards.

Now a hush fell over the audience as teachers wearing their annual colours around their shoulders walked solemnly onto the stage, parading their qualifications. They formed a black fringe at the front while green, white, lilac, gold, the erudite colours bobbed. Inside the programme, against the names, were the titles – lists of letters that meant nothing to her. She wondered if she could manage to peep from the corner of her eyes to get a look at the woman on her left to check that she was not doing anything wrong.

In the boxes and the good seats at the front, sat the VIPs and distinguished people. She wondered what their connection was with the school. They could not all have been parents singled out for favour, besides, there were too many priests among them. She felt as if she had the least right to be there. What did it matter that one of those girls was her daughter? She had handed Siobhan over to the greater institution of education.

Everyone stood up. She jumped, terrified of being slow. The headmistress was walking on stage, regal in her sweeping black habit. With a gracious gesture she showed her distinguished visitors their seats and sat down giving the cue for everyone else to sit. The staff sat, then the girls a fraction behind them. She hoped that there would not be too much getting up and sitting down. She glanced at her husband. He had found Siobhan out of the rows of faces and was smiling peacefully.

'Sixteenth row up on the right, five seats in from the centre aisle.'
She fished in her handbag for her distance glasses.
'Where? Where?'
He pointed.
'Yes,' she nodded having seen nothing.
'Look at this.' He pointed towards the programme.
She took her distance glasses off and put her reading glasses back. She hated him because he could use bifocals. The time she had tried she thought that the floor was coming up to meet her all the time and could not place her feet without worrying. She

thought that cars 400 yards away were actually on top of her and had to be helped across the roads.

He pointed to one of the names, light shining on his glasses. It was one of the teaching nuns.

'Look,' he said. 'She must be very intelligent,' and indicated with his forefinger the parade of the alphabet after her name.

Someone immediately in front turned around to look at the clock on the back wall and he coloured, imagining that they had heard him pronounce judgement. He was impressed by any outward signs of learning, and having bowed to superior knowledge found himself unable to straighten up again.

After the choir had sung various arrangements and the band had performed a scratching fugue, the guest, a young priest who had worked in the Congo, gave a speech, urging the girls to look to their reverend mother as an example of womanhood to which they should aspire. She nodded coyly, acknowledging the compliment with a graceful wave of her hand. Then she read her annual report which told of the activities the school had engaged in, the trophies they had won, the number of university entrances they had gained. They could not afford to lose one benefactor or one endowment grant. 'Look,' the report was saying, 'we are worthy of maintaining. Help to keep us afloat this year and the next . . .'

The list of prizes was being read out and the girls began to clamber down from the back of the stage to troop out and shake hands with the priest and listen to his polite congratulations. And in the middle of it was their daughter. Distinction . . . special merit . . . something or other . . . it was all a gabble to them in which the only clear thing was their child's face. Their child accepting effortlessly the warm approval of these people.

She had walked onto the stage as if she had been born to do so, slowly, taking her time. She had even turned a calm smile on the audience before returning to her seat. He thought that Siobhan had taken longer than the others had to get back to her place. She seemed to be so long on the stage, hovering, enjoying the controlled applause and hot lights. If it had been him, well, he would have run, kept his head down until he was out of the way. All those English people staring at him!

But Siobhan looked around as if she wanted to look into everyone's face and let them know that she was not scared of anyone. The hall, the school, the prizes, all belonged to her and she was at home, her confidence soaring to the upper gallery.

Sometimes he could not understand how Siobhan was their daughter. Her ways were so very different. She was so English, a foreigner to her parents. To her, Mayo was just a postmark on a card from cousins she did not know very well. If she ever brought friends home for tea he noticed how his wife grew nervous in case she did something wrong like pour the milk in first or forget to put out a jug, so that they could all tell that usually they poured straight from the bottle. She would become flustered and forget the forks, or drop things on the floor.

Siobhan saw everything and probably made excuses for her mother back at school. And when he thought that his own father had taken his teeth out to eat and set them on the table beside him. Siobhan would have been sick. Perhaps it was lucky that she had never known her grandfather, the way she complained about him for making noises when he ate. She said she could not bear it. She was sensitive and their grossness insulted her. He wondered what she said about him. Did she apologise for his accent, translate? He remembered the school elocution lessons; compulsory the letter from school had said and she had come home from them saying that they said things wrongly and correcting their speech with clipped vowels.

'RARSEBREE jam,' she had asked for in the cafe. He had nearly died.

'Go and ask for it yourself,' he had told her.

'You are saying that backwards,' she often told him with a look of disdain when he forgot and used the Irish construction. Am I not? Can I not? Amn't I?

'Are you taking Siobhan to school?' his wife would ask and he would forget the English way, that he could just say yes or no.

'I'm taking her,' he would reply.

'Why do you always answer a question by repeating it?' Siobhan asked him crossly. 'It sounds so silly.'

Not like the French, he thought. Exotic they were. Now having a French father, that would be something. Nice flowing way they have of talking, like they're singing, soft gentle sound of words. *Doucement, lentement, la vie en rose.* Not like the Irish, *nach bhfuil sé fliuch, nach bhfuil sé salach.** Eck, eck in the throat. Sounds like phlegm.

'Jesus Mary and Joseph!' was all he ever swore in English. 'Holy Mother of God! May the saints protect us!' Each time he lost his temper he called down a blessing not a curse.

*nach bhfuil sé fliuch (pron. nack wilshe fluck)—isn't it wet? nach bhfuil sé salach (pron. nack wilshe salack)—isn't it dirty?

'You sound like one of those comedians on TV,' she had said.

At the reception later, there were parents shaking hands and congratulations flowing. Their child across the room was laughing with some friends while her parents stood in a little patch of silence. But eventually it had to happen. He went up with her coat, loving, holding it open, not knowing how he was going to interrupt, he hardly dared speak.

Siobhan did not see him, she kept talking while he hovered behind her shoulder, his smile wearing him out. Gingerly he tapped her elbow.

'Come on young lady, time to leave – bid goodnight to your acquaintances.' Formal tortured speech like he had heard in the films.

He thought that he ought to help her into her coat like he had seen the men do, even James Cagney in the re-runs.

Villains held coats open, gangsters waiting for their molls.

'Come on young lady,' he repeated, wanting to help her with her coat.

Siobhan snatched it from him crossly. She blushed and put it on herself. Even she knew that certain things just were not done. Honestly, in front of her friends too! He thinks he's putting a mink wrap on her as they leave a nightclub. They had seen the same films on Sunday afternoons together. Silly old fool! You don't do that for a child!

The unspoken words rang in his head. 'I knew you would make a show of me,' as her eyes filled with hot angry tears.

Her father's gaze showed hurt, he had started to panic and she had to look away from him not wanting to see the pain in his face. She pretended it had not happened, but her friends had fallen silent, embarrassed. When she turned back she hoped he would be gone. Then her mother crossed over to where they stood knowing something was wrong. Why was he standing so stiffly, the life gone out of him and look at Siobhan, ignoring him!

'I'll slap you young madam,' she said angrily while a low moan escaped from him.

'Oh God. Not here!' and he turned and walked out down the flight of red-carpeted stairs.

Siobhan ran past, not with them, tears pouring down her face.

Don't let anyone see! Don't let anyone see!

Her back disappeared into the street . . .

Got to get out!

She followed slowly down the stairs holding the brass rail, feeling her way. Her lynch pin gone, she could trip and fall the complete flight in full view of everyone. That would never do. She called him. Some people turned around and her face felt hot and flushed. He did not hear, or if he did, he kept straight on.

God, she would kill him! And her!

Outside, on the street, Siobhan was breathing heavily. Tears of shame spilled from her eyes, despite her efforts to stop them. Later as the three walked home together in silence, each nursing their own grievance, she began thinking how much it was costing them to keep their daughter at that school. They had saved and saved to keep up with all the demands. How much were they paying for her to learn to pity them?

Divided loyalties

He felt he had lived all his life by divisions. His own country was divided.

Read

Study this information about the divisions in Northern Ireland to which Siobhan's father refers.

After many hundreds of years of English rule, in 1920 Ireland was divided into two parts, North and South. In Southern Ireland the majority of people is Catholic and in the North the majority is Protestant. In 'battle-scarred' Ulster in the North, although there are more Protestants, the Catholic minority is a significant one. Both groups have developed their own very individual cultures.

HAMISH MACDONALD *THE IRISH QUESTION*

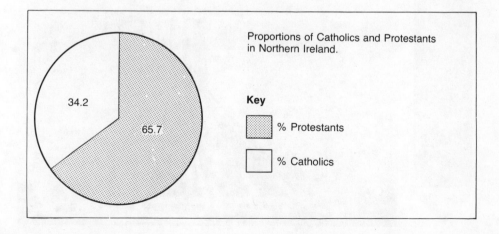

Proportions of Catholics and Protestants in Northern Ireland.

34.2

65.7

Key

% Protestants

% Catholics

More divisions

Now he lived in a divided city, torn by religion, its peoples needing
two football teams for their different loyalties.

When Irish families like Moy McCrory's emigrated to Liverpool and
London in England they inevitably took some of their divisions with
them.

Talk

In pairs, answer these questions:

● What do you learn from the story about Siobhan's father's
   background? Make notes.
● What evidence is there in the story to suggest that he wanted
   Siobhan to be educated separately from Protestant children?
● Do you think people of different religions should be educated
   separately? Explain your reasons.

The two cathedrals

At least the Anglicans had built theirs to look like a church,
somewhere to go and pray in. The plans for theirs made it look like
a space rocket.

Talk

Do you agree with Siobhan's father's description of these two
cathedrals? How important is religion to you? Explain carefully,
commenting on attitudes expressed in this story if you find it helpful.

Below and opposite, Liverpool's two cathedrals as they are today.

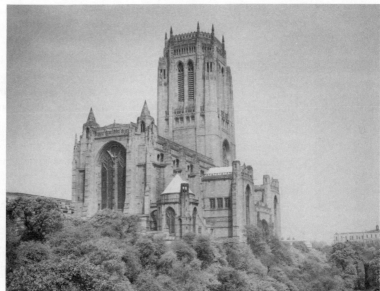

Anxious parents

Their anxieties were for themselves.

Talk

Look at the first section of the story carefully. In groups:

● List all the details you are given which describe the physical appearance of a) Siobhan's father b) her mother. For which of the two parents is more physical description given?
● For each of her parents make a list of words that best sum up how they are feeling as they walk to their daughter's school hall for the prize giving ceremony.

Family grievances

Later as the three walked home together in silence, each nursing their own grievance . . .

Talk

Study the last section carefully.

In groups, talk about why Siobhan feels that her parents have made a 'show' of her. How would you have felt in this situation?

● What were the grievances that each of the three main characters were feeling as they walked home? Describe them in as much detail as you can.

'She had walked onto the stage as if she had been born to do so, slowly, taking her time.'

Why do you think that Siobhan is so confident when she receives her prize? Why are her parents so unconfident at the prize giving? List your reasons fully and try to make clear how much of these characters' confidence is related to where they were born and how they were brought up.

● How confident would you describe yourself? When do you feel most and when least confident? Have you ever felt embarrassed at school by your parents? Why?
● In what ways do you think confidence is related to class? Give examples to support your arguments.

Assignment

Continue the story. Imagine that a full-scale argument about the events of the evening occurs when Siobhan and her parents return home.

Write it,
Either in the form of a short play
Or as three diary extracts in which each character reflects on the events of the prize giving and the family argument which followed it.

Try to concentrate on these two things:
a) the different way each of the family would write;
b) how much each member of the family might be able to understand other people's points of view.

Interview with Moy McCrory

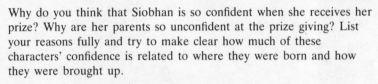

Read

Like Siobhan in *Prize Giving*, Moy McCrory came over from Ireland with her parents and went to a girls' grammar school in Liverpool.

Where did you spend your childhood?
Liverpool.

Where did you go to school?
I went to a local parish church school until I was 11, then a convent grammar school for girls in Liverpool.

What class would you say you were?
Always an awkward question: my heart and mind are working class. I have great respect for working people, for artisans, and I am suspicious of all unearned privilege. I despise the privilege of class which exists in Britain today.
   However I do not feel that to be 'working class' necessitates being uneducated, or that to remain uneducated is something to be proud of.

Moy McCrory

My mother was suspicious of all forms of learning. She never understood why I did not want to work full time in Woolworths (where I had a Saturday job while I was at school). She saw no point in education – only if it guaranteed a better job at the end of the day – which it didn't and can't and isn't the purpose of.

I think what separates people classwise is their attitude to struggle. I grew up having to struggle, having all the odds pitched against me. My education was wrested from the state, not given as a right. At home there were riots about my staying on at school, my family did not see the validity of exams.

I had to struggle at school, because naturally it was hard to fit in – I had no role models.

At college and university I became aware of the differences in the backgrounds of students. I was painfully aware that I was there because of state assistance, no one in my family could ever have helped me financially and at the end of term I could never return to the 'bosom of my family'. . .

But, possibly because of our 'Irishness', we had a great solid background of something that went beyond the everyday surface of life; call it religion, call it culture, God alone knows. But we could recite old myths, my mother was musical, she was a storyteller of great skill. My father was an inventor. There was a wonderful creative spirit in my family, which I'm very proud of. So it was not all doom and gloom.

Coming from my background I had to be resilient: nothing would ever be made easy for me. I've had to struggle against an overwhelming sense of 'class inferiority' which besets us in Britain –

it works on an insidious level, so that rationally we know it is fake, but emotionally it makes itself felt. It makes us awkward, less confident, less socially able to deal with others, and I feel we should resist these feelings. . .

At what age do you think you began to grow away from your parents?
In my early teens.

How true to your own experience is this story?
Quite close. It describes the school I went to and how awkward my parents were and how aware of this I became.

Can you say why you decided to write about this particular incident?
Not really. I had a particular sadness about it which I couldn't explain. I wanted to say 'thank you' to my own parents, to celebrate that while they never acknowledged the importance of education directly, indirectly they did. They worked hard to pay for a ridiculously expensive school uniform. It was a great sacrifice for me to go there. It was going to change me and move me away from them and they were aware of this, yet still let me go.

How important to this story is the idea of class?
It's central to it.

There is much shame in this story. The girl is ashamed of her parents, they are ashamed of themselves. How much of this is the natural awkwardness of parents and their children during adolescence?
A great deal is natural awkwardness, but for a working-class kid, this becomes intensified, because 'class' plays into these normal areas and distorts them. Nowhere are we told to be proud of ourselves. In fact we are encouraged to abandon our backgrounds as soon as we can, not to own them, to become ashamed.

The saddest thing happened when I was teaching. A colleague of mine told no one that his father was a British Railways signalman, because he thought it was too embarrassing. He let people think his father was dead, rather than claim his background. It was his strategy for survival and had been while he was a student.

Talk

- Why do you think Moy's colleague kept quiet about his father's job as a signalman?
- The author says that the story is quite close to her own experiences. What does the interview tell us about her parents that is **not** in the story?
- The author describes the idea of 'class' as being 'central' to the story. What do you find out about her own class from the interview?

● Why do you think she found it hard to 'fit in' at school?
● 'I've had to struggle against an overwhelming sense of "class inferiority" which besets us in Britain'. What do you think Moy McCrory means by 'class inferiority'? Do you think we are very class-conscious in Britain?
● Talk about what you have found most interesting in this interview.

Assignment

Interview an adult of your choice about her/his education and upbringing.

Stage 1   Prepare a list of questions. Remember that you will want your interviewee to say more than yes or no.

Stage 2   Tape-record the interview. As you are interviewing, encourage your interviewee to talk by asking helpful 'follow-up' questions.

Stage 3   Write the interview out as a script. When you do this, you may want to do some editing, removing some repetitions or hesitations, but as far as possible keep to what your interviewee was trying to say. To check that you have recorded what they meant, send them a copy of your transcript.

Bright Thursdays

Olive Senior

Thursday was the worst day. While she had no expectations of any other day of the week, every Thursday turned out to be either very good or very bad, and she had no way of knowing in advance which one it would be. Sometimes there would be so many bad Thursdays in a row that she wanted to write home to her mother, 'Please please take me home for I cannot stand the clouds'. But then she would remember her mother saying, 'Laura this is a new life for you. This is opportunity. Now dont let yu mama down. Chile, swallow yu tongue before yu talk lest yu say the wrong thing and dont mek yu eye big for everything yu see. Dont give Miss Christie no cause for complain and most of all, let them know you have broughtuptcy.'

Miss Christie was the lady she now lived with, her father's mother. She didn't know her father except for a photograph of him on Miss Christie's bureau where he was almost lost in a forest of photographs of all her children and grandchildren all brown skinned with straight hair and confident smiles on their faces. When she saw these photographs she understood why Miss Christie couldn't put hers there. Every week as she dusted the bureau, Laura looked at herself in the mirror and tried to smile with the confidence of those in the photographs, but all she saw was a being so strange, so far removed from those in the pictures, that she knew that she could never be like them. To smile so at a camera one had to be born to certain things – a big house with heavy mahogany furniture and many rooms, fixed mealtimes, a mother and father who were married to each other and lived together in the same house, who would chastise and praise, who would send you to school with the proper clothes so you would look like, be like everyone else, fit neatly into the space Life had created for you.

But even though others kept pushing her, and she tried to ease, to work her way into that space too, she sometimes felt that Life had played her tricks, and there was, after all, no space allotted for her. For how else could she explain this discomfort, this pain it caused her in this her father's house to confront even the slightest event. Such as sitting at table and eating a meal.

In her mother's house she simply came in from school or wherever and sat on a stool in a corner of the lean-to kitchen or on the steps while Mama dished up a plate of food which one ate with whatever implement happened to be handy. Mama herself would more often than not stand to eat, sometimes out of the pot, and the boys too would sit wherever their fancy took them. Everything would be black from the soot from the fireside which hung now like grotesque torn ribbons from the roof. After the meal, Laura would wash the plates and pots in an enamel basin outside the sweep out the ashes from the fireside. A meal was something as natural as breathing.

But here in this house of her father's parents a meal was a ritual, something for which you prepared yourself by washing your hands and combing your hair and straightening your dress before approaching the Table. The Table was in the Dining Room and at least twelve could have comfortably sat around it. Now Laura and the grandparents huddled together at one end and in the sombre shadows of the room, Laura sometimes imagined that they so unbalanced the table that it would come toppling over on to them. At other times, when she polished the mahogany she placed each of the children of the household at a place around this table, along with their mother and father and their bewhiskered and beribboned grandparents who looked down from oval picture frames. When they were all seated, they fitted in so neatly in their slots that there was now no place left for her. Sometimes she didn't mind.

But now at the real mealtimes, the ghosts were no longer there and she sat with the old people in this empty echoing space. Each time she sat down with dread in her heart, for meal time was not a time to eat so much as a time for lessons in Table Manners.

First Mirie the cook would tinkle a little silver bell that would summon them to the dining room, and the house would stir with soft footsteps scurrying like mice and the swish of water in the basin. All the inhabitants of the house were washing and combing and straightening themselves in preparation for the Meal. She tried not to be the last one to the table for that was an occasion for chastisement. Then she had to remember to take the stiffly starched white napkin from its silver ring and place it in her lap.

'Now sit up straight, child. Don't slump so,' Miss Christie would say as she lifted the covers off tureens. Miss Christie sat at the table uncovering dishes of food, but by the time Laura was served, her throat was already full and she got so confused that she would forget the knife and start to eat with her fork.

'Now dear, please use your knife. And don't cut your meat into little pieces all at once.'

At the sulky look which came over Laura's face, Miss Christie would say, 'You'll thank me for this one day you know, Laura. If you are going to get anywhere, you must learn how to do things properly. I just can't imagine what your mother has been doing with you all this time. How a child your age can be so ignorant of the most elementary things is beyond me.'

The first time Miss Christie had mentioned her mother in this way, Laura had burst into tears and fled from the room. But now, remembering her mother's words, she refused to cry.

Laura's father had never married her mother. The question never came up for, said Myrtle without even a hint of malice in her voice, 'Mr Bertram was a young man of high estate. Very high estate'. She was fond of telling this to everyone who came to her house and did not know the story of Laura's father. How Mr Bertram had come visiting the Wheelers where Myrtle was a young servant. They had had what she liked to call 'a romance' but which was hardly even imprinted on Mr Bertram's mind, and Laura was the result. The fact that Mr Bertram was a man of 'high estate' had in itself elevated Miss Myrtle so far in her own eyes that no one else could understand how she could have managed to bear her sons afterwards for two undoubtedly humble fathers.

Laura had come out with dark skin but almost straight hair which Miss Myrtle did her best to improve by rubbing it with coconut oil and brushing it every day, at the same time rubbing cocoa butter into her skin to keep it soft and make it 'clear'. Miss Myrtle made the child wear a broad straw hat to keep off the sun, assuring her that her skin was 'too delicate'.

Miss Myrtle had no regrets about her encounter with Mr Bertram even though his only acknowledgement of the birth was a ten dollar note sent to her at the time. But then he had been shipped off to the United States by his angry parents and nothing further had been heard of him.

Miss Myrtle was unfortunate in her choice of fathers for her children for none of them gave her any support. She single-handedly raised them in a little house on family land and took in sewing to augment what she got from her cultivation of food for the pot and ginger for the market. She did not worry about the fate of her sons for they were after all, boys, and well able to fend for themselves when the time came. But her daughter was a constant source of concern to her, for a child with such long curly hair, with such a straight nose, with such soft skin (too bad it was so dark) was surely destined for a life of ease and comfort. For years, Miss Myrtle sustained herself with the fantasy that one day Laura's father would miraculously appear and take her off to live up to the station in life to which she was born. In the meantime she groomed her daughter for the role she felt she would play in life, squeezing things here and there in order to have enough to make her pretty clothes so that she was the best-dressed little girl for miles around. For the time being, it was the only gift of her heritage that she could make her.

Then after so many years passed that it was apparent even to Myrtle that Mr Bertram had no intention of helping the child, she screwed up her courage, aided and abetted by the entire village it seemed, and wrote to Mr Bertram's parents. She knew them well, for Mr Bertram's mother was Mrs Wheeler's sister and in fact came from a family that had roots in the area.

> Dear Miss Kristie
> Greetings to you in Jesus Holy Name I trust that this letter will find that you an Mister Dolfy ar enjoin the best of helth. Wel Miss Kristie I write you this letter in fear and trimblin for I am the Little One and you are the Big One but I hope you wil not take me too forrard but mr. Bertram little girl now nine year old and bright as a button wel my dear Mam wish you could see her a good little girl and lern her lesson wel she would far in Life if she could have some Help but I am a Poor Woman! With Nothing! To Help I am in the filds morning til night. I can tel you that in looks she take after her Father but I am not Asking Mr Bertram for anything I know. He have his Life to live for but if you can fine it in Your Power to do Anything for the little girl God Richest Blessing wil come down on You May the Good Lord Bles and Keep you Miss Kristie also Mas Dolfy. And give you a long Life until you find Eternal Rest Safe in the arms of the Savor
> Your Humble Servant
> Myrtle Johnstone.

The letter caused consternation when it was received by the old people for they had almost forgotten about what the family referred to as 'Bertram's Mistake' and they thought that the woman had forgotten about it too. Although Myrtle was only 17 at the time and their son was 28, they had never forgiven what Miss Christie called the uppity black gal for seducing their son. 'Dying to raise their colour all of them,' Miss Christie had cried, 'dying to raise their colour. That's why you can't be too careful with them'. Now like a ghost suddenly materialising they could see this old scandal coming back to haunt them.

At first the two old people were angry, then as they talked about the subject for days on end, they soon dismissed their first decision which was to ignore the letter, for the little girl, no matter how

common and scheming her mother was, was nevertheless family
and something would have to be done about her. Eventually they
decided on limited help – enough to salve their consciences but not
too much so that Myrtle would get the idea that they were a limitless
source of wealth. Miss Christie composed the first of her brief and
cool letters to the child's mother.

> Dear Myrtle,
> In response to your call for help we are sending a little money
> for the child, also a parcel which should soon arrive. But
> please don't think that we can do this all the time as we
> ourselves are finding it hard to make ends meet. Besides,
> people who have children should worry about how they are
> going to support them before they have them.
> Yours Truly,
> Mrs C. Watson

They made, of course, no reference to the child's father who was
now married and living in New Jersey.

Myrtle was overjoyed to get the letter and the parcel for they were
the tangible indications that the child's family would indeed rescue
her from a life of poverty in the mountains. Now she devoted even
more care and attention to the little girl, taking pains to remind her
of the fineness of her hair, the straightness of her nose, and the
high estate of her father. While she allowed the child to continue to
help with the chores around the house, she was no longer sent on
errands. When all the other children were busy minding goats,
fetching water or firewood, all of these chores in her household now
fell on Laura's brothers. Myrtle was busy grooming Laura for a
golden future.

Because of her mother's strictures, the child soon felt alienated
from others. If she played with other children, her mother warned
her not to get her clothes dirty. Not to get too burnt in the sun. Not
to talk so broad. Instead of making her filled with pride as her
mother intended, these attentions made the child supremely
conscious of being different from the children around her, and she
soon became withdrawn and lacking in spontaneity.

Myrtle approved of the child's new quietness as a sign of 'quality'
in her. She sent a flood of letters to Miss Christie, although the
answers she got were meagre and few. She kept her constantly
informed of the child's progress in school, of her ability to read so
well, and occasionally made the child write a few sentences in the
letter to her grandmother to show off her fine handwriting. Finally,
one Christmas, to flesh out the image of the child she had been

building up over the years, she took most of the rat-cut coffee money and took the child to the nearest big town to have her photograph taken in a professional studio.

It was a posed, stilted photograph in a style that went out of fashion thirty years before. The child was dressed in a frilly white dress trimmed with ribbons, much too long for her age. She wore long white nylon socks and white T-strap shoes. Her hair was done in perfect drop curls, with a part to the side and two front curls caught up with a large white bow. In the photograph she stood quite straight with her feet together and her right hand stiffly bent to touch an artificial rose in a vase on a rattan table beside her. She did not smile.

Her grandparents, who were the recipients of a large framed print on matte paper, saw a dark-skinned child with long dark hair, a straight nose, and enormous, very serious eyes. Despite the fancy clothes, everything about her had a countrified air except for the penetrating eyes which had none of the softness and shyness of country children. Miss Christie was a little embarrassed by this gift, and hid the picture in her bureau drawer for it had none of the gloss of the photos of her children and grandchildren which stood on her bureau. But she could not put the picture away entirely; something about the child haunted her and she constantly looked at it to see what in this child was of her flesh and blood. The child had her father's weak mouth, it seemed, though the defiant chin and the bold eyes undoubtedly came from her mother. Maybe it was the serious, steady, unchildlike gaze that caused Miss Christie sometimes to look at the picture for minutes at a time as if it mesmerised her. Then she would get hold of herself again and angrily put the picture back into the drawer.

Despite her better judgement, Miss Christie found herself intensely curious about this child whose mother made her into such a little paragon and whose eyes gazed out at the world so directly.

Soon, she broached the subject obliquely to her husband. One evening at dusk as the two of them sat on the verandah, she said, 'Well, just look at the two of us. Look how many children and grandchildren we have, and not a one to keep our company'.

'Hm. So life stay. Once your children go to town, country too lonely for them after that.'

'I suppose so. But it really would be nice to have a young person about the house again.' They dropped the subject then, but she kept bringing it up from time to time.

Finally she said, as if thinking about it for the first time, 'But Dolphie, why don't we get Myrtle's little girl here?'

'What! And rake up that old thing again? You must be mad.'

'But nobody has to know who she is.'

'Then you don't know how ol'nayga fas'. They bound to find out.'

'Well, they can't prove anything. She doesn't have our name. She bears her mother's name.'

They argued about it on and off for weeks, then finally they decided to invite the child to stay for a week or two.

When Laura came, she was overawed by the big house, the patrician old couple who were always so clean and sweet-smelling as if perpetually laundered each day anew by Mirie the cook. She fell even more silent, speaking only when spoken to, and then in a low voice which could hardly be heard.

Miss Christie was gratified that she was so much lighter than the photograph (indeed, Myrtle had quarrelled with the photographer for just this reason) and although she was exactly like a country mouse, she did fill the house with her presence. Already Miss Christie was busy planning the child's future, getting her into decent clothes, correcting her speech, erasing her country accent, teaching her table manners, getting her to take a complete bath every day – a fact which was so novel to the child who came from a place where everyone bathed in a bath pan once a week since the water had to be carried on their heads one mile uphill from the spring.

In the child Miss Christie saw a lump of clay which held every promise of being moulded into something satisfactory. The same energy with which Miss Christie entered into a 'good' marriage, successfully raised six children and saw that they made good marriages themselves, that impelled her to organise the Mothers Union and the School Board – that energy was now to be expended on this latest product which relatives in the know referred to as 'Bertram's stray shot'.

Although her husband fussed and fumed, he too liked the idea of having a child in the house once more though he thought her a funny little thing who hardly made a sound all day, unlike the boisterous family they had reared. And so, as if in a dream, the child found herself permanently transported from her mother's two-room house to this mansion of her father's.

Of course her father was never mentioned and she only knew it was him from the photograph because he had signed it. She gazed often at this photograph, trying to transmute it into a being of flesh and blood from which she had been created, but failed utterly. In fact, she was quite unable to deduce even the smallest facet of his character from the picture. All that she saw was a smiling face that in some indefinable way looked like all the faces in the other photographs. All were bland and sweet. In none of these faces were there lines, or frowns, or blemishes, or marks of ugliness such as a squint eye, or a broken nose, or kinky hair, or big ears, or broken teeth which afflicted all the other people she had known. Faced with such perfection, she ceased to look at herself in the mirror.

She had gone to live there during the summer holidays and Miss Christie took every opportunity to add polish to her protegé whom she introduced everywhere as 'my little adopted'. As part of the child's education, Miss Christie taught her to polish mahogany furniture and to bake cakes, to polish silver and clean panes of glass, all of which objects had been foreign to the child's former upbringing.

The child liked to remain inside the house which was cool and dark and shaded for outside, with its huge treeless lawn and beyond, the endless pastures, frightened her.

She had grown up in a part of the mountain cockpits where a gravel road was the only thing that broke the monotony of the humpbacked and endless hills everywhere. There were so many hills that for half of the day their house and yard were damp and dark and moss grew on the sides of the clay path. It was only at midday when the sun was directly overhead that they received light. The houses were perched precariously up the hillsides with slippery paths leading to them from the road, and if anyone bothered to climb to the tops of the hills, all they would see was more mountains. Because it was so hilly the area seemed constantly to be in a dark blue haze, broken only by the occasional hibiscus or croton and the streams of brightly coloured birds dashing through the foliage. They were hemmed in by the mountains on all sides and Laura liked it, because all her life was spent in space that was enclosed and finite, protecting her from what dangers she did not even know.

And then, from the moment she had journeyed to the railway station some ten miles away and got on to the train and it had begun to travel through the endless canefields, she had begun to feel afraid. For suddenly the skies had opened up so wide all around her; the sun beat down and there was the endless noisy clacking of the train wheels. She felt naked and anxious, as if suddenly exposed, and there was nowhere to hide.

When she got off the train at the other end, there were no canefields there, but the land was still flat and open, for this was all rolling pastureland. Her curiosity about the herds of cattle she saw grazing in the shade of an occasional tree could not diminish the fear she felt at being so exposed.

Her father's parents' house was set on the top of a hill from where
they should see for miles in all directions. Whenever she went
outside she felt dizzy for the sky was so wide it was like being
enclosed within a huge blue bowl. The summer was cloudless. And
the hills were so far away they were lost in blue. But then summer
came to an end and it was time for her to go to school. The nearest
school was three miles away. Her grandmother, deciding that this
was too far for her to walk – though greater distances had meant
nothing in her former life – had arranged for her to travel to and
from school on the bus which went by at the right time each day.
This single fact impressed her most as showing the power and
might of her grandmother.

She was glad of the bus for she did not want to walk alone to
school. Now the clear summer days were ending, the clouds had
begun to gather in the sky, fat cumulus clouds that travelled in
packs and in this strange and empty country became ugly and
menacing. They reminded her of the pictures she used to get in
Sunday School showing Jesus coming to earth again, floating down
on one of these fat white clouds. And because the Jesus of their
church was a man who had come to judge and punish sinners,
these pictures only served to remind her that she was a sinner and
that God would one day soon appear out of the sky flashing fire
and brimstone to judge and condemn her. And until he came, the
clouds were there to watch her. For why else did they move,
change themselves, assume shapes of creatures awesome and
frightful, if not to torment her with her unworthiness? Sometimes
when she stood on the barbecue and looked back at the house
outlined against the sky, the house itself seemed to move and she
would feel a wave of dizziness as if the whole earth was moving
away off course and leaving her standing there alone in the
emptiness.

She would run quickly inside and find Miss Christie or Mirie or
somebody. As long as it was another human being to share the
world with.

While all day long she would feel a vague longing for her mother
and brothers and all the people she had known since childhood,
she never felt lonely, for if her mother had given her nothing else, in
taking her out of one life without guaranteeing her placement in the
next, she had unwittingly raised her for a life of solitude. Here in this
big house she wandered from room to room and said nothing all
day, for now her lips were sealed from shyness. To her newly
sensitised ears, her words came out flat and unmusical and she
would look with guilt at the photographs and silently beg pardon for

being there.

There were no other children around the house and she was now so physically removed from others that she had no chance to meet anyone. Sometimes she would walk down the driveway to the tall black gate hoping that some child would pass along and talk so that they could be friends, but whenever anyone happened by, her shyness would cause her to hide behind the stone pillar so they would not see her. And although her grandmother said nothing on the subject, she instinctively knew after a while that she would never in this place find anyone good enough to bring into Miss Christie's house.

Although she liked the feeling of importance it gave her to get on and off the bus at the school gate – the only child to do so – most times she watched with envy the other children walking home from school, playing, yelling, and rolling in the road. They wore no shoes and she envied them this freedom, for her feet, once free like theirs except for Sundays, were now encased in socks and patent leather shoes handed down from one or the other of the rightful grandchildren who lived in Kingston or New York.

Most days the bus was on time. Every morning she would wait by the tall black gate for the bus to arrive. The bus would arrive on time every day. Except Thursday. Sometimes on Thursdays the bus wouldn't arrive until late evening. She would nevertheless every Thursday go to the gates and wait, knowing in her heart that the bus would not come. Miss Christie would sometimes walk out and stand by the gate and look the road up and down.

Sometimes Mass Dolphie passing on his way from one pasture to the next would rein in his horse and would also stand by the gate and look up the road. All three would stand silently. The road swayed white in an empty world. The silence hummed like telegraph wires. Her life hung in the air waiting on a word from Miss Christie. Her chest began to swell like a balloon getting bigger and bigger. 'The bus isn't coming. You'll have to walk,' Miss Christie pronounced with finality.

'Oh Miss Christie, just a few minutes more,' she begged. It was the only thing she begged for. But she knew that the bus wouldn't come, and now, at this terribly late hour, she would have to walk alone the three miles to school in a world that was empty of people. She would walk very fast, the dust of the marl road swirling round her ankles, along this lonely road that curved past the graveyard. Above, following every step of the way, the fat clouds sat smirking and smug in the pale blue sky. She hated them for all they knew about her. Her clumsiness, her awkwardness, the fact that she did not belong in this light and splendid place. They sat there in judgement on her every Thursday. Thursday, the day before market day. The day of her Armageddon.

Thursdays the old bus would sit on the road miles above, packed with higglers and their crocus bags, bankras and chickens. The bus would start right enough: somewhere on the road above the bus would start in the dawn hours, full and happy. And then, a few miles after, the bus would gently shudder and like a torn metal bird would ease to a halt with a cough and a sigh and settle down on the road, too tired and worn out to move. It would remain there until evening, the market women sitting in the shade and fanning the flies away with the men importantly gathered around the machine, arguing and cursing until evening when the earth was cool again and the driver would go slowly, everything patched up till next Thursday when the higglers descended with their crocus bags and their bankras, their laughter and their girth and their quarrelling and their ferocious energy which would prove too much for the old bus. Then with a sigh it would again lie still on the road above her. Every Thursday.

Sometimes though if she managed to dawdle long enough Miss Christie would say, 'Heavens, It's 10 o'clock. You can't go to school again'.

'O Miss Christie' she would cry silently 'thank you, thank you'.

Sometimes when she didn't go to school Mass Dolphie would let her dig around in his Irish potato patch collecting the tiny potatoes for herself.

Digging potatoes was safe. She could not see the sky. And she never knew when a really big potato would turn up among all the tiny ones.

'Like catching fish, eh?' Mass Dolphie said and she agreed though she didn't know how that was having never seen the sea. But she would laugh too.

II

One day they got a letter from the child's father. He was coming home with his wife on a visit. It wasn't long after their initial joy at hearing the news that the grandparents realised that difficulties were bound to arise with the child. For one thing, they hadn't told their son about her, being a little ashamed that they had not consulted him at all before coming to the decision to take her. Besides, it was a little awkward to write to him about such matters at his home, since from all they had heard of American women they believed that there was a strong possibility that his wife would open his letters.

Their immediate decision was to send the child home, but that too presented certain problems since it was still during the school term and they couldn't quite make up their minds what they would tell her mother to explain a change of heart. They certainly couldn't tell her the truth for even to them the truth seemed absurd; that they wanted to return the little girl because her father was coming. For once, Miss Christie was at a loss. It was Mr Dolphie who took a firm line. 'Write and ask him what to do,' he instructed his wife, 'after all, it's his child. If he doesn't want her here when he comes then he can tell us what we should do with her'.

They were surprised but not overly so when their son wrote that they should do nothing about the child as he would be greatly amused to see her.

Mr Dolphie didn't see any cause for amusement in the situation and thought that it was just like his youngest son to take a serious thing and make a joke of it and all in all act in a reckless and irresponsible manner. He had certainly hoped that Bertram had finally settled down to the seriousness of life.

Long before they told the child the news of her father's coming, she knew, for without deliberately listening to their conversations, she seemed to absorb and intuitively understand everything that happened in the house.

Since hearing the news there had been a joy in her heart, for her mother had told her so often that one day this mysterious father of hers would come and claim her as his own that she had grown to believe it. She knew that he would come and rescue her from fears as tenuous as clouds and provide her with nothing but bright Thursdays.

But when she searched out the photograph from the ones on the bureau, his face held that unreadable, bland smile and his eyes gave off nothing that would show her just how he intended to present his love for her.

One day Miss Christie said to her, 'Laura, our son is coming on a visit. Mr Bertram'. She said it as if the child and the man bore no relationship to each other. 'He is coming with his wife. We haven't seen him for so many years'.

Yes. Since I was born, Laura thought.

'Now Laura, I expect you to be on your best behaviour when they are here.'

'Yes mam.'

Laura showed no emotion at all as Miss Christie continued to chat on the subject. How does one behave with a father? Laura thought. She had no experience of this. There were so few fathers among all the people she knew.

Miss Christie turned the house upside down in a frenzy of preparation for her son's visit. Without being told so, Laura understood that such preparation was not so much for the son as for his white wife. She was quite right, for as Miss Christie told Mirie, 'these foreign women are really too fresh, you know. Half of them don't really come from anywhere but they believe that everybody from Jamaica is a monkey and lives in trees. I am really glad my son is bringing her here so that she can see how we live'. Laura silently assented to that, for who in the wide world could keep up a life that was as spotless and well ordered as Miss Christie's?

Laura longed to talk to somebody about her father. To find out what he was really like. But she did not want to ask Miss Christie. She thought of writing secretly to her mother and telling her that Mr Bertram was coming, asking what he was really like, but she was too timid to do anything behind Miss Christie's back for Miss Christie was so all-knowing she was bound to find out. Sometimes she wanted to ask Mirie the cook who had been working with the family for nearly forty years. But although she got into the habit of dropping into the roomy kitchen and sitting at the table there for hours, she never got up the nerve to address Mirie, and Mirie, a silent and morose woman, never addressed her at all. She believed, though, that Mirie liked her, for frequently, without saying a word, she would give her some titbit from the pot, or a sample of the cookies, or bread and guava jelly, though she knew that Miss Christie did not approve of eating between meals. But apart from grunting every now and then as she went about her tasks, Mirie said nothing at all on the subject of Mr Bertram or any other being. Laura wished that Mirie would talk to her, for she found the kitchen the most comforting part of the house.

Her father and his wife arrived one day when she was at school. When she got home, she was too shy to go in, and was hanging around trying to hide behind a post when Miss Christie spotted her. 'Oh Laura, come and meet my son,' said Miss Christie and swept her into the living room. 'Mina,' she said to a yellow-haired woman sitting there, 'this is Laura, the little adopted I was telling you about'. Laura first vaguely made out the woman, then Mass Dolphie, then a strange man in the shadows, but she was too shy to give him more than a covert glance. He did not address her but gave a smile which barely moved his lips. In days to come she would get accustomed to that smile, which was not as bland as in the photograph. To his daughter, he paid no more attention. It was his wife who fussed over the little girl, asking questions and exclaiming over her curls. Laura could hardly understand anything the woman said, but was impressed at how trim and neat she was, at the endless fascination of her clothes, her jewellery, her laughter, her accent, her perfume, her assurance. Looking at her long polished nails, Laura had a picture of her mother's hands, the nails cracked and broken like a man's from her work in the fields; of her mother's dark face, her coarse shrill voice. And she was bitterly ashamed. Knowing the mother she had come from, it was no wonder, she thought, that her father could not acknowledge her.

She was extremely uneasy with the guests in the house. Their presence strained to the fullest the new social graces that Miss Christie had inculcated in her. Now she had a two-fold anxiety: not to let her mother down to Miss Christie, and not to let Miss Christie down in front of this white woman from the United States of America.

For all the woman's attentions, it was the man that she wanted to attend her, acknowledge her, love her. But he never did. She contrived at all times to be near him, to sit in his line of vision, to 'accidentally' appear on the path when he went walking through the pastures. The man did not see her. He loved to talk, his voice going on and on in a low rumble like the waves of the sea she had never seen, the ash on his cigarette getting longer till it fell on his clothes or Miss Christie's highly polished floor. But he never talked to her. This caused her even greater anxiety than Miss Christie's efforts at 'polishing' her, for while she felt that Miss Christie was trying, however painful it was, to build her up, she could not help feeling that her father's indifference did nothing so much as to reduce her, nullify her. Laura would have wondered if he knew who she was if she hadn't known that Miss Christie had written to him on the subject. She decided then that all his indifference was merely part of a play, that he wanted to surprise her when he did claim her, and was working up to one magical moment of recognition that would thereafter illuminate both their lives forever and ever. In the daytime that is how she consoled herself but at nights she cried in the little room where she slept alone in the fearful shadow of the breadfruit tree against the window pane.

Then Thursday came round again and in this anxiety she even forgot about her father. As usual the bus was late and Laura hung around the gate hoping that Miss Christie would forget she was there until it was too late to walk to school. The road curved white and lonely in the empty morning, silent save for the humming of bees and the beating of her own heart. Then Miss Christie and Mina appeared on the verandah and obviously saw her. Talking together, they started to walk slowly towards the gate where she stood, trapped by several impulses. Laura's heart beat faster then almost stopped as her father appeared from the orange grove and approached the two women. Now the three of them were walking towards her. They were now near enough for Laura to hear what they were saying but her eyes were only on her father.

'Oh dear, that old bus. Laura is going to be late again,' Miss Christie said.

'Oh for chrissake. Why don't you stop fussing so much about the bloody little bastard,' her son shouted.

Laura heard no more for after one long moment when her heart somersaulted once there was no time for hearing anything else for her feet of their own volition had set off at a run down the road and by the time she got to the school gates she had made herself an orphan and there were no more clouds.

higgler – pedlar
bankras – wicker travelling basket

Who's who?

Write

A number of characters in this story have an important effect on Laura's life. In pairs, make brief notes on each of these people:

● Bertram;
● Miss Myrtle;
● Miss Christie (Mrs C. Watson);
● The Wheelers.

Eg.

The Wheelers

1. A high-class family who employed Myrtle as a young maid.
2. It was in their house that Bertram met Myrtle.

What happens when?

Talk

The story lasts a number of years but it is not told in the order in which it actually happened. Below is a list of key events. Each event has been given a letter. In pairs agree on the correct order. Copy out the time line, and write the letters of the events in that order in the empty boxes. The first and last have been done for you.

Time line: Bright Thursdays

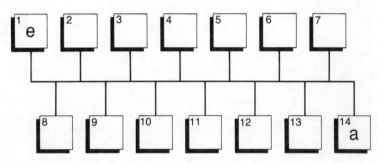

Events

a)   Laura and Bertram meet
b)   Bertram marries and settles in New Jersey
c)   'Bertram's mistake'
d)   Myrtle writes to Miss Christie
e)   Myrtle is a servant at the Wheelers
f)   Miss Christie replies to Myrtle and sends a parcel
g)   One Christmas Myrtle sends Laura's photograph to Miss Christie
h)   Bertram writes to say he is coming to visit his mother
i)   Myrtle sends 'a flood of letters'
j)   Bertram sends a ten dollar note to Myrtle
k)   Bertram is shipped to the United States of America
l)   Myrtle and Bertram's 'romance'
m)   Bertram visits the Wheelers
n)   Laura goes to live with her grandparents

Assignment

Stage 1   Decide which of these events involve Laura directly.

Stage 2   What else happens to Laura that is not included on the time line? List the events.

Stage 3   Using this information retell the story from Laura's point of view *in the order it happened*, highlighting the things that were important to her.

Parents and children

Her mother had told her so often that one day this mysterious father of hers would come and claim her as his own.

Read

Adopted children who discover their natural parents often find the experience a very powerful one.

Holly

At about one-thirty in the afternoon, the telephone rang, and the voice on the other end asked for my mother. It was a Saturday and I was home alone. I said she was out, so the caller asked me to write down her name, address, and telephone number, which I did. Then the woman who was on the other end of the phone said, 'Fourteen years ago I had a baby that I gave up for adoption. I believe you are my daughter.'

I was in total shock, and as we talked, my mind was in a different world. She asked me a lot of questions about myself and filled me in on what had happened to her. She said she was five-foot-four, had blond hair and green eyes, and that she worked for a management consulting company. And she explained why she had put me up for adoption. She was seventeen when she met and fell in love with my birthfather, but by the time she found out she was pregnant they had broken up. She wanted to keep me, but her mother talked her out of it. She told me she had gotten married since then, to someone else, but was presently divorced and she didn't have any other kids. We talked for about an hour, and after I hung up I started sobbing. One of my father's friends, Mike Rodgers, came in the door looking for my parents, and I put my arms around him and just kept on crying and crying. I couldn't stop.

I wasn't crying because I was sad. I had planned on searching when I got a little older, and my parents were going to help me. In fact, it was something we had talked about very recently. So I was happy that my birthmother had found me, but I never expected it to be so all-of-a-sudden. I always figured I had till tomorrow—you know, a few years more before I really had to deal with it.

I was finally able to tell Mike about the phone call, and he drove me over to where my mother—my adoptive mother—was working. On the way over we met my Dad, but I was still crying so hard I couldn't explain what had happened—I couldn't get the words out of my mouth. He thought someone had died until I was finally able to tell him, and then he didn't know what to say. I had to leave for a basketball game at school, so he went and picked up Mom at work, told her to sit down, and told her everything. When I got home from the game, we all talked and decided it would be best to begin a relationship slowly—that we would just exchange information and photographs by mail for a while. That's what we did for about two months. I was still wandering around in a daze during this time, and I was worried about how my life might change. My mother said I should just think of Alison, my birthmother, as a friend, and that I should try to put myself in her position, so that's what I tried to do. And then in May we finally met. We invited Alison to stay with us for a few days, and she flew out for a weekend visit. My parents and I met her at the airport, and that was really weird. I was glad we were a little bit late because that gave us something to talk about while we were walking through the terminal. After we got to our house she gave me a picture of my birthfather and also the little bracelet they had put on my wrist when I was born. She had kept it all these years.

Jane

I was fifteen and it was in early December when my birthmother, Lorraine, phoned and spoke to my mother. The first time she called, Lorraine pretended she was conducting a survey for *Seventeen* magazine. It was around dinner time, and I was in the family room doing my homework. Mom was in the kitchen and I answered the phone, but the questions were a little confusing so I put my mother on the phone. Mom told the caller that I had a learning disability and she answered a couple of questions, but since she was in the middle of preparing dinner she didn't talk for very long.

That very same night, at approximately nine-thirty, the phone rang again. A woman asked to speak to my mother and I went upstairs to get ready for bed. It turned out to be the same lady who had said she was from *Seventeen*, except that this time she told my mom: 'On April 5, 1966, I gave birth to a daughter in Rochester, New York, whom I put up for adoption. I have reason to believe Jane is that child.'

Mom told Lorraine that she was glad to hear from her and they talked for about half an hour. I wasn't aware of what was going on until Daddy came into my room and told me who was on the phone. He asked me if I would like to talk to her and even though I was stunned I said yes. Lorraine and I talked for about twenty minutes and the conversation was very weird. She told me a lot about her family, but it was hard for me to concentrate and I can't remember what we really talked about. After we hung up, my parents and I talked for a while, and then about an hour later we called Lorraine back and invited her and her husband to visit with us. Lorraine mentioned she would be coming to the Midwest during the Christmas holidays, but that didn't seem like a good idea to us so we suggested she wait until January. However, the next morning Lorraine called and said she would like to fly in on Saturday morning—which was only two days away! Even though my parents felt it was a little too soon for a visit—that we needed some time to adjust to this idea—my Mom said all right because I was eager to meet my birthmother and of course she could hardly wait to meet me. She had worked so hard to find me, we could easily imagine how excited she was.

For the next couple of days, we all spent a lot of time talking and reassuring each other. My mother was especially nervous because she felt extremely threatened. She told a few close friends what was happening, and most of them were against it, saying that she was too trusting and too foolish. My friends also disapproved and said things like 'I wouldn't let her just walk into your life. You should tell her to buzz off!' But we're a really close family and all of us decided we loved each other and nothing could interfere with that love.

On Saturday morning, Dad and I went to the airport to meet Lorraine's plane. I saw a woman standing there looking around, not knowing where to go, so we figured it was her. I expected her to be taller because I'm tall for my age. She gave me a big hug, but I didn't know how to react so I kept my hands in my pockets. I felt a little awkward. In the car she asked me a lot of questions like what were my favourite subjects and what did I like to do. It seemed like having another grandmother visit because she was asking all those routine grandmother questions.

We spent the whole weekend at our house, mostly talking, and we showed each other photographs. Lorraine had brought a lot of family pictures with her, and I showed her several albums of my childhood. We stayed at home all day Saturday, and on Sunday we went to church and walked around the shopping centre. One of the things we talked about—and giggled over—is that we had both spent hours deciding what we should wear for our big meeting. As it turned out, I wore jeans and she wore slacks.

Lorraine left on Monday morning after a nice visit and I went back to school. Later that month, the day after Christmas, I flew out to Detroit by myself to meet Lorraine's family and I stayed two days. Lorraine actually lives in New York, but her mother lives in Detroit, which is why we got together there. It was the first time I'd ever been on a plane, so I was probably as thrilled about that as anything else. They had a big family gathering which included Lorraine's husband, her mother, her two brothers, and lots of other relatives, but I was too overwhelmed by it and felt uncomfortable. Everyone treated me like a relative, which bothered me because I didn't feel that way. At one point, someone who was talking to me referred to Lorraine as 'your Mom' and I didn't like that at all and said so. If I hadn't said anything I would have felt guilty and that wouldn't have helped anyone in the long run.

JILL KREMENTZ *HOW IT FEELS TO BE ADOPTED*

Talk

Compare the experiences of Laura, Holly and Jane. In what ways are they similar, in what ways different?

Should adopted children be encouraged to find and meet their natural parents? What are the arguments for and against such meetings? List them in two separate columns.

Assignment

Either Write a story about an adopted child who meets his or her natural parent(s) for the first time;
Or Write a story set in a society in which children choose their parents. Describe how you come to choose yours.

Minding your manners

Meal time was not a time to eat so much as a time for lessons in Table Manners.

Read

Different classes have different styles of behaviour, particularly when it comes to eating. Look at this advice from the *Observer* on how to behave at a dinner party.

- The napkin should be unfolded to make a long strip, placed across the knees (never tucked into your front). Apart from wiping drips from your chin (which shouldn't be necessary), it stays there until you dump it unfolded on the table at the end of the meal. It is only folded if you are a house guest and napkin rings have been provided.
- Finger bowls are placed above the forks when food is eaten with the fingers. Dip the tips of your fingers in the water, brush them across the lemon if there is some, and discreetly dry them on your napkin. If a finger bowl arrives on your fruit plate, put it in position yourself, usually with the lace mat it is sitting on.
- The difficulty of balancing peas on the convex side of a fork means that forks are turned over, more and more. This is now almost acceptable, provided it is done elegantly and the food pushed on to the *inner* edge. But many people still regard it as 'kitchen manners' for family only.
- A soup spoon, unlike a knife, should be held rather like a pen, but the wrist turned so the spoon faces across the body and is parallel to the table. The soup is then quietly sipped from the *side* of the spoon as you tilt it towards the mouth. You don't blow on it, nor do you put the spoon in your mouth. Then, as the soup gets low in the bowl, tilt it away from you, and if you cannot lift a spoonful to your mouth without dripping, lightly brush the drips from the back of the spoon against the further edge of the bowl, before lifting it to your mouth.
- A pudding or cereal spoon is used in rather the same way. But if a pudding is served on a plate, a small fork must *always* be used to help the food on to the spoon.

For the Good Guest

- Always look to see how many helpings will be needed from a dish before helping yourself, and adjust your portion accordingly – though without looking as if you are *counting* the peas, however few there are.

- If you have to get rid of a bone or other debris, raise your fork or spoon to your mouth and *discreetly* eject the offending morsel. Then slip it neatly on to the side of your plate – tucking it under other leftovers if it is something which might embarrass the hostess. When eating fruit with your fingers, a stone can be ejected into the hole formed by the thumb and forefinger of a lightly clenched fist, then placed on the plate.
- Don't put your own knives, forks or spoons into serving dishes.
- It's 'not done' to handle food which others are going to eat – so don't check the peaches for ripeness or pick up hard cheese to cut it.
- Don't play 'mother' at other people's dinner tables and 'helpfully' serve other people with food – unless they ask you to.
- Don't make noises. The worst example I have seen of this was someone who put whole baby crabs into his mouth and extruded the shells on to his plate, in a continuous stream as he munched.
- Don't smoke between courses.

● Don't automatically stack plates to help the hostess clear away. Look to see what she does. If she takes the plates off individually do the same. In the early 1950s there was a *Punch* cartoon of a wife at a dining table turning to her husband and saying 'Do we stack or are we gentry?' An allusion to the fact that, lacking staff, only those who clung determinedly to their pre-war standards continued to carry the plates off one at a time after family meals.
● Don't reach for more drink, unless you have been told to help yourself, and *never* put the bottle on the floor beside you.

Talk

● Who would use this advice?
● How relevant is it to you?
● Study the ways in which Laura's eating habits are changed by her grandmother. What do you think her grandmother's 'rules' might have been. List them.
● 'You'll thank me for this one day, Laura' her grandmother tells her. Why do you think Miss Christie insists on changing Laura? Do you think she has Laura's best interests at heart?
● In what ways do you think codes of behaviour like the one described above can be used to make people feel uncomfortable?
● How important are good manners to you? Is there a difference between good manners and the rules in the article?
● What would you include in your own list of good manners for
   a)   eating?
   b)   behaviour?

Assignment

Produce a guide to modern manners for teenagers. Include the following sections:

● How to behave at school – staff and students, in and out of classrooms;
● How to behave at home – parents, guardians, brothers, sisters;
● How to behave when you are out – friends, older or younger people, people in authority.

Throughout your guide, try not to include 'rules' which would make anyone feel ashamed of their origins.

The Stolen Party

Liliana Heker

As soon as she arrived she went straight to the kitchen to see if the monkey was there. It was: what a relief! She wouldn't have liked to admit that her mother had been right. *Monkeys at a birthday?* her mother had sneered. *Get away with you, believing any nonsense you're told!* She was cross, but not because of the monkey, the girl thought; it's just because of the party.

'I don't like you going,' she told her. 'It's a rich people's party.'

'Rich people go to Heaven too,' said the girl, who studied religion at school.

'Get away with Heaven,' said the mother. 'The problem with you, young lady, is that you like to fart higher than your ass.'

The girl didn't approve of the way her mother spoke. She was barely nine, and one of the best in her class.

'I'm going because I've been invited,' she said. 'And I've been invited because Luciana is my friend. So there.'

'Ah yes, your friend,' her mother grumbled. She paused. 'Listen, Rosaura,' she said at last. 'That one's not your friend. You know what you are to them? The maid's daughter, that's what.'

Rosaura blinked hard: she wasn't going to cry. Then she yelled: 'Shut up! You know nothing about being friends!'

Every afternoon she used to go to Luciana's house and they would both finish their homework while Rosaura's mother did the cleaning. They had their tea in the kitchen and they told each other secrets. Rosaura loved everything in the big house, and she also loved the people who lived there.

'I'm going because it will be the most lovely party in the whole world, Luciana told me it would. There will be a magician, and he will bring a monkey and everything.'

The mother swung around to take a good look at her child, and pompously put her hands on her hips.

'Monkeys at a birthday?' she said. 'Get away with you, believing any nonsense you're told!'

Rosaura was deeply offended. She thought it unfair of her mother to accuse other people of being liars simply because they were rich. Rosaura too wanted to be rich, of course. If one day she managed to live in a beautiful palace, would her mother stop loving her? She felt very sad. She wanted to go to that party more than anything else in the world.

'I'll die if I don't go,' she whispered, almost without moving her lips.

And she wasn't sure whether she had been heard, but on the morning of the party she discovered that her mother had starched her Christmas dress. And in the afternoon, after washing her hair, her mother rinsed it in apple vinegar so that it would be all nice and shiny. Before going out, Rosaura admired herself in the mirror, with her white dress and glossy hair, and thought she looked terribly pretty.

Señora Ines also seemed to notice. As soon as she saw her, she said:

'How lovely you look today, Rosaura'.

Rosaura gave her starched skirt a slight toss with her hands and walked into the party with a firm step. She said hello to Luciana and asked about the monkey. Luciana put on a secretive look and whispered into Rosaura's ear: 'He's in the kitchen. But don't tell anyone, because it's a surprise.'

Rosaura wanted to make sure. Carefully she entered the kitchen and there she saw it: deep in thought, inside its cage. It looked so funny that the girl stood there for a while, watching it, and later, every so often, she would slip out of the party unseen and go and admire it. Rosaura was the only one allowed into the kitchen. Señora Ines had said: 'You yes, but not the others, they're much too boisterous, they might break something.' Rosaura had never broken anything. She even managed the jug of orange juice, carrying it from the kitchen into the dining-room. She held it carefully and didn't spill a single drop. And Señora Ines had said: 'Are you sure you can manage a jug as big as that?' Of course she could manage. She wasn't a butterfingers, like the others. Like that blond girl with the bow in her hair. As soon as she saw Rosaura, the girl with the bow had said:

'And you? Who are you?'

'I'm a friend of Luciana,' said Rosaura.

'No,' said the girl with the bow, 'you are not a friend of Luciana because I'm her cousin and I know all her friends. And I don't know you.'

'So what,' said Rosaura. 'I come here every afternoon with my mother and we do our homework together.'

'You and your mother do your homework together?' asked the girl, laughing.

'I and Luciana do our homework together,' said Rosaura, very seriously.

The girl with the bow shrugged her shoulders.

'That's not being friends,' she said. 'Do you go to school

together?'

'No.'

'So where do you know her from?' said the girl, getting impatient.

Rosaura remembered her mother's words perfectly. She took a deep breath.

'I'm the daughter of the employee,' she said.

Her mother had said very clearly: 'If someone asks, you say you're the daughter of the employee; that's all.' She also told her to add: 'And proud of it.' But Rosaura thought that never in her life would she dare say something of the sort.

'What employee?' said the girl with the bow. 'Employee in a shop?'

'No,' said Rosaura angrily. 'My mother doesn't sell anything in any shop, so there.'

'So how come she's an employee?' said the girl with the bow.

Just then Señora Ines arrived saying *ssh ssh*, and asked Rosaura if she wouldn't mind helping serve out the hot-dogs, as she knew the house so much better than the others.

'See?' said Rosaura to the girl with the bow, and when no one was looking she kicked her in the shin.

Apart from the girl with the bow, all the others were delightful. The one she liked best was Luciana, with her golden birthday crown; and then the boys. Rosaura won the sack race, and nobody managed to catch her when they played tag. When they split into two teams to play charades, all the boys wanted her for their side. Rosaura felt she had never been so happy in all her life.

But the best was still to come. The best came after Luciana blew out the candles. First the cake. Señora Ines had asked her to help pass the cake around, and Rosaura had enjoyed the task immensely, because everyone called out to her, shouting 'Me, me!' Rosaura remembered a story in which there was a queen who had the power of life or death over her subjects. She had always loved that, having the power of life or death. To Luciana and the boys she gave the largest pieces, and to the girl with the bow she gave a slice so thin one could see through it.

After the cake came the magician, tall and bony, with a fine red cape. A true magician: he could untie handkerchiefs by blowing on them and make a chain with links that had no openings. He could guess what cards were pulled out from a pack, and the monkey was his assistant. He called the monkey 'partner.' 'Let's see here, partner,' he would say, 'Turn over a card.' And, 'Don't run away, partner: time to work now.'

The final trick was wonderful. One of the children had to hold the monkey in his arms and the magician said he would make him disappear.

'What, the boy?' they all shouted.

'No, the monkey!' shouted back the magician.

Rosaura thought that this was truly the most amusing party in the whole world.

The magician asked a small fat boy to come and help, but the small fat boy got frightened almost at once and dropped the monkey on the floor. The magician picked him up carefully, whispered something in his ear, and the monkey nodded almost as if he understood.

'You mustn't be so unmanly, my friend,' the magician said to the fat boy.

'What's unmanly?' said the fat boy.

The magician turned around as if to look for spies.

'A sissy,' said the magician. 'Go sit down.'

Then he stared at all the faces, one by one. Rosaura felt her heart tremble.

'You, with the Spanish eyes,' said the magician. And everyone saw that he was pointing at her.

She wasn't afraid. Neither holding the monkey, nor when the magician made him vanish; not even when, at the end, the magician flung his red cape over Rosaura's head and uttered a few magic words. . .and the monkey reappeared, chattering happily, in her arms. The children clapped furiously. And before Rosaura returned to her seat, the magician said:

'Thank you very much, my little countess.'

She was so pleased with the compliment that a while later, when her mother came to fetch her, that was the first thing she told her.

'I helped the magician and he said to me, "Thank you very much, my little countess."'

It was strange because up to then Rosaura had thought that she was angry with her mother. All along Rosaura had imagined that she would say to her: 'See that the monkey wasn't a lie?' But instead she was so thrilled that she told her mother all about the wonderful magician.

Her mother tapped her on the head and said: 'So now we're a countess!'

But one could see that she was beaming.

And now they both stood in the entrance, because a moment ago Señora Ines, smiling, had said: 'Please wait here a second.'

Her mother suddenly seemed worried.

'What is it?' she asked Rosaura.

'What is what?' said Rosaura. 'It's nothing; she just wants to get the presents for those who are leaving, see?'

She pointed at the fat boy and at a girl with pigtails who were also waiting there, next to their mothers. And she explained about the presents. She knew, because she had been watching those who left before her. When one of the girls was about to leave, Señora Ines would give her a bracelet. When a boy left, Señora Ines gave him a yo-yo. Rosaura preferred the yo-yo because it sparkled, but she didn't mention that to her mother. Her mother might have said: 'So why don't you ask for one, you blockhead?' That's what her mother was like. Rosaura didn't feel like explaining that she'd be horribly ashamed to be the odd one out. Instead she said:

'I was the best-behaved at the party.'

And she said no more because Señora Ines came out into the hall with two bags, one pink and one blue.

First she went up to the fat boy, gave him a yo-yo out of the blue bag, and the fat boy left with his mother. Then she went up to the girl and gave her a bracelet out of the pink bag, and the girl with the pigtails left as well.

Finally she came up to Rosaura and her mother. She had a big smile on her face and Rosaura liked that. Señora Ines looked down at her, then looked up at her mother, and then said something that made Rosaura proud:

'What a marvellous daughter you have, Herminia.'

For an instant, Rosaura thought that she'd give her two presents: the bracelet and the yo-yo. Señora Ines bent down as if about to look for something. Rosaura also leaned forward, stretching out her arm. But she never completed the movement.

Señora Ines didn't look in the pink bag. Nor did she look in the blue bag. Instead she rummaged in her purse. In her hand appeared two bills.

'You really and truly earned this,' she said handing them over. 'Thank you for all your help, my pet.'

Rosaura felt her arms stiffen, stick close to her body, and then she noticed her mother's hand on her shoulder. Instinctively she pressed herself against her mother's body. That was all. Except her eyes. Rosaura's eyes had a cold, clear look that fixed itself on Señora Ines's face.

Señora Ines, motionless, stood there with her hand outstretched. As if she didn't dare draw it back. As if the slightest change might shatter an infinitely delicate balance.

Translated by Alberto Manguel

Being in service

'You know what you are to them? The maid's daughter, that's what.'

Read

Although this story is set in Argentina, Rosaura's mother is in a situation that used to be common in Britain. She is a maid in a wealthy house. Read this extract from the memories of a woman who spent all her life in service.

Wealthy children were never allowed to play with low-class children like us. They were never allowed to play with anyone but similarly wealthy children. They never went anywhere on their own without their nannies. Some of them had two, a nurse and an under-nurse. The lawns were open to everybody, and they couldn't keep us away from them, but if any child wandered up to us, its nurse would say, 'Come away! Come away this instant! Come over here'. They'd never let them speak to us.

Mind you we had a kind of contempt for them. They couldn't do the things we could do. They weren't allowed to dirty their clothes like we were. They weren't allowed to run in and out of the bushes. They weren't allowed to climb all over the seats and walk along the very narrow tops of them. They weren't allowed to do anything exciting. It wasn't their fault.

So we never mixed, never. They played their dainty little games with large coloured balls. They pushed their dolls' prams around and rode on their scooters.

We had nothing except perhaps an old tennis ball, but still we used to have the most marvellous games with absolutely nothing at all.

Perhaps if we had been allowed to mix, we would have become quite friendly but I don't think so because they were a different class of people from us altogether.

For instance, I remember one occasion when I was playing on the lawns, I had a coat on which had originally been my grandmother's. It was a plush affair. One of these children came over and started making remarks about my coat. The nanny said to her, 'Oh, you shouldn't say things like that dear, after all, they're poor children. Their mummy hasn't got any money'. And the child said, 'Haw, haw, but doesn't she look funny? I wonder if Mummy has got anything she could give her to wear'. I was simply furious because I hadn't minded the coat. I hadn't felt that because it was my grandmother's coat there was something wrong about wearing it.

But although this incident has stuck in my mind I soon got over my feelings of resentment because there was always something to do or something to look forward to, like the yearly visit to the circus.

MARGARET POWELL *CLIMBING THE STAIRS*

Talk

In pairs, discuss

● The main differences between the ways 'low-class' children played and what 'wealthy' children were allowed to do;
● The similarities and differences between the situation remembered here and the one described in *The Stolen Party*;
● Whether you think children are aware of differences in class between themselves and their friends? Does it matter to you?

The world of make-believe

'I'm going because it will be the most lovely party in the whole world. . .'
'Thank you very much my little countess.'

Read

The Stolen Party is in several ways like a fairy tale. Compare this version of a tale involving another well-known party.

Cinderella

Once upon a time there lived a merchant and his wife. They were very happy together. Their greatest joy was their daughter. She was loving and good-natured. They gave her lots of toys to play with and fine clothes to wear and she too was very happy.

But one day the little girl's mother fell ill. She grew more and more sick and no doctors could save her. At last she died. Both the merchant and his daughter were very unhappy. The little girl cried herself to sleep each night.

But at last the merchant began to get over his loss. One day he decided to marry again. His new wife had two daughters of her own and at first she and her children were kind to the little girl.

But life can be cruel sometimes and one day the merchant was attacked by robbers and killed. Quite suddenly his new wife changed her behaviour towards the little girl. She began to treat her like a servant instead of like a daughter. She took away all her fine clothes and all her toys and gave them to her own children. The little girl had to wear rags. She was turned out of her room and instead she slept in the kitchen, huddled by the fire for warmth. When the stepsisters saw this they jeered at her and called her 'Cinderella'. And from then on she was always known by that name.

Although Cinderella had to wait on the stepmother and her two daughters hand and foot she never grumbled. But they complained. If things were not just right they shouted and scolded and soon their bad-temper showed in their faces. They grew uglier and uglier.

One day the stepmother came home very excited. She told her two daughters the news. The King had announced that a Grand Ball was to be held at the castle that night and every young girl in the town was invited. 'The King's son will be there,' she announced, 'and it's well known that he's looking for a wife.'

How the two ugly sisters fussed about dressing and preening themselves when they heard this news. They shouted at Cinderella to shine their shoes, paint their nails and brush their hair. When at last they were ready Cinderella spoke up hopefully. 'If every girl in the town is invited, then may I go too?'

The stepmother and her two ugly daughters roared with laughter. 'Don't be so ridiculous!' they cried. 'Look at you.' Cinderella crept away and looked at herself in a mirror. She was dressed in rags. How could she go to the Ball?

After the others had left Cinderella began to tidy up the house. As she cleared up the mess left by the ugly sisters, the tears ran down her cheeks. All of a sudden there was a flash of light and Cinderella looked up. Standing in front of her was an old lady. In her hand was a wand.

'Who are you?' gasped Cinderella.

'I am your Fairy Godmother,' said the woman. 'I have come to help you. Dry your eyes, Cinderella. You shall go to the Ball.'

The old woman waved her wand over Cinderella and the rags she was wearing changed to a beautiful ball-gown. 'Now,' said the Fairy Godmother, 'there's no time to lose. Get me the biggest pumpkin you can find'.

Cinderella did as she was told and brought a huge pumpkin from the vegetable garden. The old woman gave another wave of her magic wand and the pumpkin changed before Cinderella's eyes into a marvellous glass coach. As Cinderella stood staring at it her Fairy Godmother turned and pointed her wand at the mice that ran across the kitchen floor. There was a flash of light and instead of mice four strong horses stood tethered to the coach. And a footman stood holding the door.

'And last but by no means least. . .' said the old woman. She waved her wand a fourth time and Cinderella found herself wearing tiny glass slippers. 'Quickly,' said her Fairy Godmother, 'into the coach. But make sure you leave the Ball before midnight for when the clock stops chiming, the magic will vanish.'

Cinderella drove to the Ball in the glass coach. Everyone turned to look as she entered. They all wondered who this beautiful stranger could be. Nobody recognised her, least of all her stepmother or the two ugly sisters. The Prince could not take his eyes off her. He went over to her and asked her for a dance and as they danced together they looked deep into each other's eyes.

Cinderella was so happy she didn't notice the time pass. She was listening to the Prince tell her of life in the palace when she suddenly heard the clock striking. She looked up and saw its hands on midnight. 'I must go!' she cried and she ran from the room, down the grand staircase and out of the palace. She was in such a hurry to go that she did not notice that she had dropped one glass slipper on the way. The prince tried to follow her but she was too fast for him. Instead he picked up the glass slipper.

Next morning the Prince decided to look for Cinderella. He let it be known far and wide that he would marry the girl whose foot fitted the glass slipper. He travelled to all the houses in the town asking all the girls who lived there to try on the slipper. But it fitted none of them. At last he came to Cinderella's house. The two ugly sisters were terribly excited to see the Prince. They elbowed and pushed each other out of the way, each wanting to be first to try on the glass slipper. But though they strained as hard as they could to put it on, the slipper was much too small for either of them.

'Is there no other girl in the house who might try it on?' the Prince asked.

'Only Cinderella,' they said. 'It is not worth letting her try it on.'

But the Prince insisted. Shyly, Cinderella came forward, dressed in

her rags. The Prince held the slipper and Cinderella put her foot forward. It fitted perfectly. There was a gasp of dismay from the stepmother and her two daughters and a cry of joy from the Prince, for as he looked into her eyes he realised that here was his beautiful dancing partner. 'The wedding shall be this very day,' he said.

The whole town was invited to the wedding, even the stepmother and her two ugly daughters, for Cinderella was not the sort of person to bear malice. There was feasting and merry-making, singing and dancing, and from that day onwards Cinderella and the Prince lived happily every after.

Talk

In groups, consider these statements and decide how much you agree with them.

- Cinderella's situation is just like Rosaura's.
- Cinderella's situation is nothing like Rosaura's.
- The magician is like the Prince in *Cinderella*.
- Rosaura's mother is an ugly sister.
- Rosaura is treated like a princess at the party.
- Rosaura is treated like a servant at the party.
- Life was cruel for Cinderella and Rosaura.
- Rosaura was quite intelligent enough to find a husband without having to use a Fairy Godmother.
- Mothers always know best.
- Rosaura didn't live happily ever after.
- Rosaura would probably have lived happily ever after.
- Being the maid's daughter was worse than having a lousy stepmother.
- The two stories are nothing like each other at all.

Assignment

Write a modern version of *Cinderella* called *The Stolen Party*.

The theft

Señora Ines didn't look in the pink bag. Nor did she look in the blue bag. Instead she rummaged in her purse. In her hand appeared two bills.

Talk

Imagine you were Rosaura. How do you think you would have felt if you were offered money and not a bracelet? Explain your reasons.

Imagine you were Señora Ines. Why did you give Rosaura money and not a present? How did she seem to react? Did you regret your decision to give her money? Why?

In what ways does Rosaura disapprove of her mother? Explain this fully, with evidence from the story.

What has Rosaura learned by the end of this story?

What is the 'infinitely delicate balance' of this story. What is 'balanced'? What has this to do with class? With being young?

The title of this story is *The Stolen Party*. In what ways is the party 'stolen'? List all the ways in which you think this title might apply. Has anything else been stolen? If so, how and what?

Assignment

Write a short story which includes the following ingredients:

● characters: two or more characters of clearly different backgrounds;
● setting: set in one place at an event of some kind;
● situation: exploring a situation to do with money.

The Martyr

Ngugi wa Thiongo

When Mr and Mrs Garstone were murdered in their home by unknown gangsters, there was a lot of talk about it. It was all on the front pages of the daily papers and figured importantly in the Radio Newsreel. Perhaps this was so because they were the first European settlers to be killed in the increased wave of violence that had spread all over the country. The violence was said to have political motives. And wherever you went, in the market-places, in the Indian bazaars, in a remote African duka, you were bound to hear something about the murder. There were a variety of accounts and interpretations.

Nowhere was the matter more thoroughly discussed than in a remote, lonely house built on a hill, which belonged, quite appropriately, to Mrs Hill. Her husband, an old veteran settler of the pioneering period, had died the previous year after an attack of malaria while on a visit to Uganda. Her only son and daughter were now getting their education at 'Home' – home being another name for England. Being one of the earliest settlers and owning a lot of land with big tea plantations sprawling right across the country, she was much respected by the others if not liked by all.

For some did not like what they considered her too 'liberal' attitude to the 'natives'. When Mrs Smiles and Mrs Hardy came into her house two days later to discuss the murder, they wore a look of sad triumph – sad because Europeans (not just Mr and Mrs Garstone) had been killed, and of triumph, because the essential depravity and ingratitude of the natives had been demonstrated beyond all doubt. No longer could Mrs Hill maintain that natives could be civilized if only they were handled in the right manner.

Mrs Smiles was a lean, middle-aged woman whose tough, determined nose and tight lips reminded one so vividly of a missionary. In a sense she was. Convinced that she and her kind formed an oasis of civilization in a wild country of savage people, she considered it almost her calling to keep on reminding the natives and anyone else of the fact, by her gait, talk and general bearing.

Mrs Hardy was of Boer descent and had early migrated into the country from South Africa. Having no opinions of her own about anything, she mostly found herself agreeing with any views that most approximated those of her husband and her race. For instance, on this day she found herself in agreement with whatever

Mrs Smiles said. Mrs Hill stuck to her guns and maintained, as indeed she had always done, that the natives were obedient at heart and *all* you needed was to treat them kindly.

'That's all they need. *Treat them kindly*. They will take kindly to you. Look at my "boys". They all love me. They would do anything I ask them to!' That was her philosophy and it was shared by quite a number of the liberal, progressive type. Mrs Hill had done some liberal things for her 'boys'. Not only had she built some brick quarters (*brick*, mind you) but had also put up a school for the children. It did not matter if the school had not enough teachers or if the children learnt only half a day and worked in the plantations for the other half; it was more than most other settlers had the courage to do!

'It is horrible. Oh, a horrible act,' declared Mrs Smiles rather vehemently. Mrs Hardy agreed. Mrs Hill remained neutral.

'How could they do it? We've brought 'em civilization. We've stopped slavery and tribal wars. Were they not all leading savage miserable lives?' Mrs Smiles spoke with all her powers of oratory. Then she concluded with a sad shake of the head: 'But I've always said they'll never be civilized, simply can't take it.'

'We should show tolerance,' suggested Mrs Hill. Her tone spoke more of the missionary than Mrs Smiles's looks.

'Tolerant! Tolerant! How long shall we continue being tolerant? Who could have been more tolerant than the Garstones? Who more kind? And to think of all the squatters they maintained!'

'Well, it isn't the squatters who. . .'

'Who did? Who did?'

'They should all be hanged!' suggested Mrs Hardy. There was conviction in her voice.

'And to think they were actually called from bed by their houseboy!'

'Indeed?'

'Yes. It was their houseboy who knocked at their door and urgently asked them to open. Said some people were after him –'

'Perhaps there –'

'No! It was all planned. All a trick. As soon as the door was opened, the gang rushed in. It's all in the paper.'

Mrs Hill looked away rather guiltily. She had not read her paper.

It was time for tea. She excused herself and went near the door and called out in a kind, shrill voice.

'Njoroge! Njoroge!'

Njoroge was her 'houseboy'. He was a tall, broad-shouldered man nearing middle age. He had been in the Hills' service for more than ten years. He wore green trousers, with a red cloth-band round the waist and a red fez on his head. He now appeared at the door and raised his eyebrows in inquiry – an action which with him accompanied the words, 'Yes, Memsahib?' or 'Ndio, Bwana'.

'Leta Chai.'

'Ndio, Memsahib!' and he vanished back after casting a quick glance round all the Memsahibs there assembled. The conversation which had been interrupted by Njoroge's appearance was now resumed.

'They look so innocent,' said Mrs Hardy.

'Yes. Quite the innocent flower but the serpent under it.' Mrs Smiles was acquainted with Shakespeare.

'Been with me for ten years or so. Very faithful. Likes me very much.' Mrs Hill was defending her 'boy'.

'All the same I don't like him. I don't like his face.'

'The same with me.'

Tea was brought. They drank, still chatting about the death, the government's policy, and the political demagogues who were undesirable elements in this otherwise beautiful country. But Mrs Hill maintained that these semi-illiterate demagogues who went to Britain and thought they had education did not know the true aspirations of their people. You could still win your 'boys' by being kind to them.

Nevertheless, when Mrs Smiles and Mrs Hardy had gone, she brooded over that murder and the conversation. She felt uneasy and for the first time noticed that she lived a bit too far from any help in case of an attack. The knowledge that she had a pistol was a comfort.

Supper was over. That ended Njoroge's day. He stepped out of the light into the countless shadows and then vanished into the darkness. He was following the footpath from Mrs Hill's house to the workers' quarters down the hill. He tried to whistle to dispel the silence and loneliness that hung around him. He could not. Instead he heard a bird cry, sharp, shrill. Strange thing for a bird to cry at night.

He stopped, stood stock-still. Below, he could perceive nothing. But behind him the immense silhouette of Memsahib's house – large, imposing – could be seen. He looked back intently, angrily. In his anger, he suddenly thought he was growing old.

'You. You. I've lived with you so long. And you've reduced me to this!' Njoroge wanted to shout to the house all this and many other things that had long accumulated in his heart. The house would not respond. He felt foolish and moved on.

Again the bird cried. Twice!

'A warning to her,' Njoroge thought. And again his whole soul rose in anger – anger against those with a white skin, those foreign elements that had displaced the true sons of the land from their God-given place. Had God not promised Gekoyo all this land, he and his children, forever and ever? Now the land had been taken away.

He remembered his father, as he always did when these moments of anger and bitterness possessed him. He had died in the struggle – the struggle to rebuild the destroyed shrines. That was at the famous 1923 Nairobi Massacre when police fired on a people peacefully demonstrating for their rights. His father was among the people who died. Since then Njoroge had had to struggle for a living – seeking employment here and there on European farms. He had met many types – some harsh, some kind, but all dominating, giving him just what salary they thought fit for him. Then he had come to be employed by the Hills. It was a strange coincidence that he had come here. A big portion of the land now occupied by Mrs Hill was the land his father had shown him as belonging to the family. They had found the land occupied when his father and some of the others had temporarily retired to Muranga owing to famine. They had come back and *Ng'o*! the land was gone.

'Do you see that fig tree? Remember that land is yours. Be patient. Watch these Europeans. They will go and then you can claim the land.'

He was small then. After his father's death, Njoroge had forgotten this injunction. But when he coincidentally came here and saw the tree, he remembered. He knew it all – all by heart. He knew where every boundary went through.

Njoroge had never liked Mrs Hill. He had always resented her complacency in thinking she had done so much for the workers. He had worked with cruel types like Mrs Smiles and Mrs Hardy. But he always knew where he stood with such. But Mrs Hill! Her liberalism was almost smothering. Njoroge hated settlers. He hated above all what he thought was their hypocrisy and complacency. He knew that Mrs Hill was no exception. She was like all the others, only she loved paternalism. It convinced her she was better than the others. But she was worse. You did not know exactly where you stood with her.

All of a sudden, Njoroge shouted, 'I hate them! I hate them!' Then a grim satisfaction came over him. Tonight, anyway, Mrs Hill would die – pay for her own smug liberalism, her paternalism and pay for all the sins of her settler race. It would be one settler less.

He came to his own room. There was no smoke coming from all

the other rooms belonging to the other workers. The lights had even gone out in many of them. Perhaps, some were already asleep or gone to the Native Reserve to drink beer. He lit the lantern and sat on the bed. It was a very small room. Sitting on the bed one could almost touch all the corners of the room if one stretched one's arms wide. Yet it was here, *here*, that he with two wives and a number of children had to live, had in fact lived for more than five years. So crammed! Yet Mrs Hill thought that she had done enough by just having the houses built with brick.

'Mzuri, sana, eh?' (very good, eh?) she was very fond of saying. And whenever she had visitors she brought them to the edge of the hill and pointed at the houses.

Again Njoroge smiled grimly to think how Mrs Hill would pay for all this self-congratulatory piety. He also knew that he had an axe to grind. He had to avenge the death of his father and strike a blow for the occupied family land. It was foresight on his part to have taken his wives and children back to the Reserve. They might else have been in the way and in any case he did not want to bring trouble to them should he be forced to run away after the act.

The other Ihii (Freedom Boys) would come at any time now. He would lead them to the house. Treacherous – yes! But how necessary.

The cry of the night bird, this time louder than ever, reached his ears. That was a bad omen. It always portended death – death for Mrs Hill. He thought of her. He remembered her. He had lived with Memsahib and Bwana for more than ten years. He knew that she had loved her husband. Of that he was sure. She almost died of grief when she had learnt of his death. In that moment her settlerism had been shorn off. In that naked moment, Njoroge had been able to pity her. Then the children! He had known them. He had seen them grow up like any other children. Almost like his own. They loved their parents, and Mrs Hill had always been so tender with them, so loving. He thought of them in England, wherever that was, fatherless and motherless.

And then he realized, too suddenly, that he could not do it. He could not tell how, but Mrs Hill had suddenly crystallized into a woman, a wife, somebody like Njeri or Wambui, and above all, a mother. He could not kill a woman. He could not kill a mother. He hated himself for this change. He felt agitated. He tried hard to put himself in the other condition, his former self and see her as just a settler. As a settler, it was easy. For Njoroge hated settlers and all Europeans. If only he could see her like this (as one among many white men or settlers) then he could do it. Without scruples. But he could not bring back the other self. Not now, anyway. He had never thought of her in these terms. Until today. And yet he knew she was the same, and would be the same tomorrow – a patronizing, complacent woman. It was then he knew that he was a divided man and perhaps would ever remain like that. For now it even seemed an impossible thing to snap just like that ten years of relationship, though to him they had been years of pain and shame. He prayed and wished there had never been injustices. Then there would never have been this rift – the rift between white and black. Then he would never have been put in this painful situation.

What was he to do now? Would he betray the 'Boys'? He sat there, irresolute, unable to decide on a course of action. If only he had not thought of her in human terms! That he hated settlers was quite clear in his mind. But to kill a mother of two seemed too painful a task for him to do in a free frame of mind.

He went out.

Darkness still covered him and he could see nothing clearly. The stars above seemed to be anxiously waiting Njoroge's decision. Then, as if their cold stare was compelling him, he began to walk, walk back to Mrs Hill's house. He had decided to save her. Then probably he would go to the forest. There, he would forever fight with a freer conscience. That seemed excellent. It would also serve as a propitiation for his betrayal of the other 'Boys'.

There was no time to lose. It was already late and the 'Boys' might come any time. So he ran with one purpose – to save the woman. At the road he heard footsteps. He stepped into the bush and lay still. He was certain that those were the 'Boys'. He waited breathlessly for the footsteps to die. Again he hated himself for this betrayal. But how could he fail to hearken to this other voice? He ran on when the footsteps had died. It was necessary to run, for if the 'Boys' discovered his betrayal he would surely meet death. But then he did not mind this. He only wanted to finish this other task first.

At last, sweating and panting, he reached Mrs Hill's house and knocked at the door, crying, 'Memsahib! Memsahib!'

Mrs Hill had not yet gone to bed. She had sat up, a multitude of thoughts crossing her mind. Ever since that afternoon's conversation with the other women, she had felt more and more uneasy. When Njoroge went and she was left alone she had gone to her safe and taken out her pistol, with which she was now toying. It was better to be prepared. It was unfortunate that her husband had died. He might have kept her company.

She sighed over and over again as she remembered her

pioneering days. She and her husband and others had tamed the wilderness of this country and had developed a whole mass of unoccupied land. People like Njoroge now lived contented without a single worry about tribal wars. They had a lot to thank the Europeans for.

Yes she did not like those politicians who came to corrupt the otherwise obedient and hard-working men, especially when treated kindly. She did not like this murder of the Garstones. No! She did not like it. And when she remembered the fact that she was really alone, she thought it might be better for her to move down to Nairobi or Kinangop and stay with friends a while. But what would she do with her boys? Leave them there? She wondered. She thought of Njoroge. A queer boy. Had he many wives? Had he a large family? It was surprising even to her to find that she had lived with him so long, yet had never thought of these things. This reflection shocked her a little. It was the first time she had ever thought of him as a man with a family. She had always seen him as a servant. Even now it seemed ridiculous to think of her houseboy as a father with a family. She sighed. This was an omission, something to be righted in future.

And then she heard a knock on the front door and a voice calling out 'Memsahib! Memsahib!'

It was Njoroge's voice. Her houseboy. Sweat broke out on her face. She could not even hear what the boy was saying for the circumstances of the Garstones' death came to her. This was her end. The end of the road. So Njoroge had led them here! She trembled and felt weak.

But suddenly, strength came back to her. She knew she was alone. She knew they would break in. No! She would die bravely. Holding her pistol more firmly in her hand, she opened the door and quickly fired. Then a nausea came over her. She had killed a man for the first time. She felt weak and fell down crying, 'Come and kill me!' She did not know that she had in fact killed her saviour.

On the following day, it was all in the papers. That a single woman could fight a gang fifty strong was bravery unknown. And to think she had killed one too!

Mrs Smiles and Mrs Hardy were especially profuse in their congratulations.

'We told you they're all bad.'

'They are all bad,' agreed Mrs Hardy. Mrs Hill kept quiet. The circumstances of Njoroge's death worried her. The more she thought about it, the more of a puzzle it was to her. She gazed still into space. Then she let out a slow enigmatic sigh.

'I don't know,' she said.

'Don't know?' Mrs Hardy asked.

'Yes. That's it. Inscrutable.' Mrs Smiles was triumphant. 'All of them should be whipped.'

'All of them should be whipped,' agreed Mrs Hardy.

The background

They were the first European settlers to be killed in the increased wave of violence that had spread all over the country.

Read

Study this information carefully.

The Martyr is set in Kenya during the revolt by the native African people against the white settlers who ruled them. These events are normally referred to as Mau Mau and lasted from the late 1940s up to 1963 when Kenya became independent. To understand the story fully it is helpful to have a fuller picture of the background.

Significant dates in Kenyan history relating to Mau Mau

1880s	The arrival of white settlers.
1920s	Kenya becomes a 'Colony'. In Nairobi political organisations begin to be formed to resist the European attempts to cut African wages, to seek improvements in education and to remove the colour barrier. In 1923 police kill Africans who are peacefully demonstrating for their rights. In the rural areas protest centres on land rights.
1930s	Growing political activity relating to land issues and squatters' rights.
1940s	Political movements seeking African majority rule develop.
1946	First use of Freedom oaths.
1948	First reference to Mau Mau by an official report.
1952	State of emergency declared as violence grows. Jomo Kenyatta and other leaders arrested.
1952/6	The Mau Mau emergency. Violent nationalist activities throughout Kenya.
1960	Emergency officially ended.
1960/3	Transfer from colonial rule to majority rule ending with election of Jomo Kenyatta as President of Kenya.

M. LIKIMANI

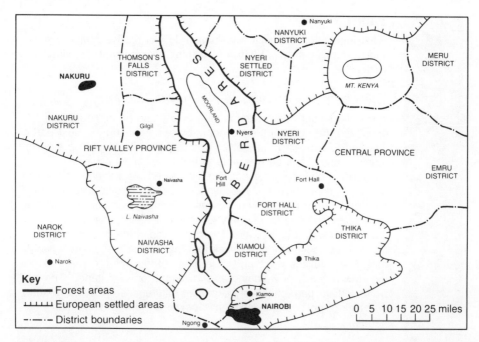

Colonial Kenya

White settler's home in Kenya

Talk

What impression of Ngugi wa Thiongo do you receive from the story and from this extract? What do you think he felt about the white settlers?

The conflict according to Ngugi wa Thiongo

The white settler came early in the century and he immediately controlled the heart of the economy by appropriating the best part of the land to himself...The settler was told that this would be a white man's country, and he was able to use his political power to consolidate his economic position. He forced black men into labour gangs, working for him...He rationalized this exploitation of African land and labour by claiming he was civilizing a primitive people. The government and the missionary aided the settler in this belief. That the African was a child was a basic premise: if the African wanted a share in the government, he was told that he had yet to grow. He had to acquire the ways and style of life of the white man – through the slow process of watching and imitating from a distance. The white settler, then, effectively exploited differences in culture to keep the reins of political and economic power out of the black man's hands.

What is Ngugi wa Thiongo saying in this extract about the behaviour of white settlers in Kenya? How true is this of

● Mrs Smiles and Mrs Hardy
● Mrs Hill?

A squatter childhood

Since then Njoroge had had to struggle for a living – seeking employment here and there on European farms.

Read

Read the following extract by Kavari Njami.

My father was born on the Kikuyu Reserve in a section of the country called *Nyeri*, where his fathers had lived for many years before him. Soon after he had gone through the traditional initiation ceremony called *irua* which made him a fully fledged man, he went westward to the 'land of the strangers', seeking his fortune on a European farm. He had visions of prosperity—a little money and many goats. The young men had been coming back to the Reserve telling of how easy it was to become 'rich' in the Great Rift Valley. So my father and other ambitious men bade their kinsmen goodbye and set out to become Squatters.

Squatter system was introduced into Kenya as a result of European settlement in the highlands. It can be defined as a form of modified neo-feudalism whereby a European farmer would permit several Africans to farm on small strips or plots of land, growing only enough food to live on, in return for labour on the European farm. In addition to these small strips of land some European farmers used to pay their Squatters some six to eight shillings a month. Some, too, offered their Squatters large plots or smaller, depending on the discretion of the European farmer concerned. Squatters had to work long hours, from seven in the morning to five in the evening.

Evacuees from the fighting

A Squatter's life was very frustrating, uncertain, and miserable. For example, there were no medical facilities available for the Squatters, no recreation of any kind, and no schools were encouraged for the children of the Squatters, though certain isolated European farmers did permit some Christian Squatters to build churches near their villages on the farm. There were also a very few individual settlers who had allowed their Squatters to operate small elementary schools at which some Squatter children could learn to read and write in their vernacular languages, and very elementary arithmetic.

The idea was, not to encourage too much education for the Squatter children as they were meant to replace their fathers on the farms when their fathers were too old to work on them. Hence, a Squatter's child could only look forward to becoming a Squatter like his father. Some lucky Squatters could send some of their children to the Kikuyuland to get some education. This process was encouraged after the Second World War, particularly. European settlers were not supposed to know all this. For it was feared that if they did, those who sent their children to get an education away in the Kikuyu Country might be dismissed by their European bosses.

Another peculiar aspect of the Squatter system was that whatever important product was grown by the Squatters on their small plots of land was to be sold to the European farmer who owned the land at a price fixed by him. Other small products were allowed to be sold on the local markets or to the Indian merchants directly. Corn was one of the major products which the Squatters had to sell to their European farmers only.

KAVARI NJAMI *A SQUATTER CHILDHOOD*

Talk

What were the main features of a squatter's life according to Kavari Njami? In what ways was his lifestyle similar to that of Njoroge?

A settler's childhood

She sighed over and over again as she remembered her pioneering days.

Read

Now read this account of colonial Kenya which takes a different point of view. (It comes from Arnold Curtis' [ed] *Memories of Kenya*.)

I remember trudging over the uneven ground of the low-lying vleiland, up the gentle slope, until we reached the plateau which made up the floor of the larger of the two valleys. There we were met by Kipsigis men, bearing gifts of chicken and eggs.

To me, unused to the ways of Africans, this welcome was strangely touching, and throughout the years I have never failed to be amazed at the generous way Africans give of the little they have. I realize now that they were men who were already squatting with their families on the 1,300 acres we had bought, and so, hoping they could remain, it was in their interests to placate the new owners; but whatever the motive, it was a kindly gesture, and since that day I have liked and trusted the Kipsigis, who were our friends and neighbours for many years.

Our task that September day long ago was to choose the site for our house. This was not easy, for in some places the grass was over our heads which made it difficult to see what the land was like. It would have been unwise to choose a low-lying site, because of the danger of malaria, but it was equally foolish to go too far up the hillside, knowing that we should have to cart all our water from the stream below.

At last a site was chosen and pegged out, and it has proved to be an excellent choice. The bungalow we built there, a long low house with a thatched roof, a cross between an African hut and a Devonshire cottage, nestles under the protection of Kipkebe Hill. The house sits on a little raised terrace of lawn, supported by a dry stone wall, edged with gay herbaceous borders. An open verandah does duty for the front entrance. From there you look over brightly coloured flower beds to the cool green lawns below, now edged with great trees of our own planting. Kipkebe was occupied by our family, after it was built in 1929, for thirty-six years.

In those early days farms were almost entirely run by squatter labour under a sort of Feudal System which, although it had many disadvantages, possessed one great advantage outweighing all else: namely the bond that was created between the European farmer and his African employees. To your squatters you were father and mother, and responsible for the physical well-being not only of the man himself but of his wife and family. This made the relationship between master and man a much more personal one, and although under a bad employer the system was open to abuse, on the whole it worked well.

By law, squatters were allowed to cultivate one acre of land, keep ten head of cattle and twenty goats. In return they were expected to work for six months in every year, and the farmer could also call on them and their families in times of emergency, to fight a bush fire or some other threatened disaster. However, it was seldom that the contract was observed to the letter, and what they were supposed to have on paper bore no relation to what they had in practice. Every squatter would soon be the proud possessor of two or three huts, the same number of wives, and in a very short time there were hundreds of head of livestock on the back portion of the farm, where the bush was literally alive with children, cattle, goats and sheep.

After a few years of this regime, our Kipsigis squatters were farming half our land! But as long as we did not need the back valley we did not mind, for their cattle and goats kept down the bush, and they cleared the land to plant their shambas (cultivated plots). The disadvantages were that they cut down all the timber to build their houses, make their cattle bomas, and to provide firewood, and that their primitive methods of cultivation harmed the land; but these disadvantages were far outweighed by the advantage to a young farmer with limited capital of having to hand a cheap labour force over whom he had some control.

So for more than twelve years, while we lived, worked, played and had our being in the front valley, our African squatters worked for us, but lived, played, and with their wives and livestock had their being in the back valley, where the population of man and beast increased daily in the most alarming fashion.

Thus in the Twenties life at Kipkebe flowed along, and nothing upset the even tenor of our ways, although Pax Britannica was rudely shattered now and then by tribal wars.

So frequently did these 'wars' break out—almost every week—that they were looked upon as an annoyance rather than a danger. For it was very inconvenient if, after one of these forays, your entire labour force was absent without leave on Monday morning, being incarcerated in the local gaol. Given any option by the District Commissioner, the farmer always plumped for a fine all round, rather than a prison sentence.

The war-cry, a high-pitched wail made by the women, might be heard at any hour of day or night, whenever they wanted to collect the tribe for some purpose ranging from a full-scale attack to a leopard hunt, or even a burglary. A dismal sound even in broad daylight, on a moonlight night the effect of the cry echoing through the hills was eerie in the extreme.

Talk

Look at the information given in this extract and the short story.

● Make a list of the first tasks facing a new white settler arriving in Kenya. What would have been most unlike life in Britain?

● How did the settlers think of the African people?
● Look back to what Ngugi wa Thiongo had to say about the conflict in Kenya. In what ways are his accusations against the white settlers proved or disproved by this account?

Freedom Boys' oath

Read

Young men who joined the organisations which fought against British rule in Kenya swore oaths of secrecy. Below is an example of one of these.

Mau Mau fighters being rounded-up

I swear before God and before all the people present here that. . .

1 I shall never reveal this secret of the KCA oath – which is of Gikuyu and Mumbi and which demands land and freedom – to any person who is not a member of our society. If I ever reveal it, may this oath kill me! (Repeated after each vow while biting the chest of a billy goat held together with the heart and lungs.)

2 I shall always help any member of our society who is in difficulty or need of help.

3 If I am ever called, during the day or night, to do any work for this society, I shall obey.

4 I shall on no account ever disobey the leaders of this society.

5 If I am ever given firearms or ammunition to hide, I shall do so.

6 I shall always give money or goods to this society whenever called upon to do so.

7 I shall never sell land to a European or an Asian.

8 I shall not permit intermarriage between Africans and the white community.

9 I will never go with a prostitute.

10 I shall never cause a girl to become pregnant and leave her unmarried.

11 I will never marry and then seek a divorce. . . . . .

Talk

● Which of the lines in the Freedom Boys' oath do you think might have had most influence on Njoroge in the story?

● Having read some of what was involved in an oath of this kind, how would you describe the beliefs of The Freedom Boys?

Assignment

Producing a Reader's Guide.

  Using the information you have studied and anything else that you can find out, prepare some background notes on *The Martyr* suitable for a student of your own age studying this story.

Stage 1 Identify words or ideas which you did not know on first reading the story, for example,

settler   *natives*   *squatters*   *Freedom Boys*   etc.

Stage 2 Make rough notes on each of these, looking up information in a dictionary or library if necessary.

Stage 3 Prepare a list of characters in the stories and make brief notes on

a) who they are, and

b) what part they play.

Stage 4 Divide the information in your notes into headings of your own, deciding what piece of explanation or summarised information you would put under each. Try to remember the reader you are writing for and what would be most helpful to them.

Stage 5 Present your background information as attractively as possible in pamphlet form.

Njoroge's dilemma

What was he to do now? Would he betray the 'Boys'? He sat there, irresolute, unable to decide on a course of action.

Talk

● In pairs, go through the story noting any information relating to the relationship between Mrs Hill and Njoroge.

● List all the possible reasons Njoroge could have had for hating Mrs Hill.

● In what ways might Njoroge have seen Mrs Hill as different from other settlers?

- What were the reasons which Njoroge finally realised prevented him from killing Mrs Hill?
- What do you think you would have done in Njoroge's position? Explain your reasons.

Read

Ngugi wa Thiongo has written this about violence.

Violence in order to change an intolerable unjust social order is not savagery: it purifies man. . . .In Kenya we were confronted with two forms of violence on the African people for fifty years. In 1952, once the political leaders were arrested and detained, the colonial regime intensified its acts of indiscriminate terrorism, thereby forcing many peasants and workers to take to the forests. For about four years, these people, with little experience of guerilla warfare, without help from any outside powers, organised themselves and courageously resisted the British military forces.

NGUGI WA THIONGO

Talk

- What do you think Ngugi means by saying that violence *purifies* man?
- Do you think violence is ever justified? If so, explain why you think so and give examples of any situations which you feel support your argument.

Homes and homelessness

'Do you see that fig tree? Remember that land is yours. Be patient. Watch these Europeans. They will go and then you can claim the land.'

Read

The land in this story used to 'belong' to Njoroge's family until Mr and Mrs Hill arrived.

Njoroge's experience of being deprived of his home was shared by many other Kenyans who were forced to become squatters. Read Karari Njami's memory of this.

Our new home was situated on my grandfather's land, less than three hundred yards from the fringe of the Aberdare Forest. My grandmother had died long ago when my father was still a young boy. My grandfather, who was at this time over 90 (he died in 1943 when his hut caught on fire while he slept), had three sons and four daughters of which my father was the third born and second son. He was a very brave man and had a big spear, much longer and wider than the normal Kikuyu spear, which he called *kiembo*. My grandfather, because he always kept this huge spear with him, was nicknamed Kiembo. He was a big hunter and owned big land in the forests where he used to hunt. One day I was sitting down on our homestead lawn with my grandfather warming ourselves by the heat of the sun when my grandfather pointed to a small hill in the middle of the forest just above the juncture of the Gura River and the Charangatha River and asked me: 'My grandson, do you see that hill?' 'Yes, grandfather,' I replied. 'That is where I used to hunt before the arrival of the *Chomba*–the European. That hill is still called Karari's Hill. If you went there, you could see my cooking pots in my cave. I have many beehives on that hill which would yield a lot of honey. But you see, none of my sons is interested in hunting or honey collecting. I am now old and cannot go there. Oh! My beloved beehives will rot there. I wish I were younger.'

Read

This collection of facts about land is taken from the *New Internationalist*.

● Australian aborigines and North American Indians hadn't heard of the idea of land ownership until Europeans arrived.
● Australian aborigines see the land as part of their bodies; something that contains the spirits of their ancestors.
● More than half the rural population in the Third World are landless and their numbers are growing.
● In the UK 1 per cent of the population owns 52 per cent of the land; there are estimated to be 30,000 squatters in London.

NEW INTERNATIONALIST, NOVEMBER 1987

Talk

● Do your family own any land? Have they ever owned land?
● Does your family rent any land or property?
● How important is it to feel certain that your home will not be moved by someone else? Does it make any difference whether you rent or own your home, provided you know it is there?
● What part do you think Njoroge's feelings about his family's land played in shaping his attitude to white settlers? How do you think you would have felt?

Homelessness in Britain

Read

Homelessness is a growing problem for young and old in London.

Growing army of beggars in London

Stephen Cook

On a grey morning with seagulls swooping over the Thames, Barry and his dog Tripper have secured a prime begging pitch – one end of Hungerford Bridge, the central London pedestrian link between north and south banks. Commuters hurry past, dropping occasional coins in his black woolen hat.

"It's the ones who don't even look at you who make me feel angry," says Barry, a 27-year-old from Bradford with a blond beard, an earring, and sharp blue eyes. "They just blank you out. They don't have to give, but at least they could look at you and see that you're another human being.

"Some of them say things to you, like why don't you get a job, and some get pretty abusive. But what can you say back? It's degrading enough having to beg in the first place. The best givers are the poorer-looking ones – perhaps they know what it's like."

Barry is part of a growing army of beggars in the streets of the capital. Five years ago it was unusual to be accosted and asked for money on a walk round the centre, but now it is almost inevitable, and the supplicants are younger.

Barry arrived seven years ago, worked in kitchens and lived in a squat. When Southwark council reclaimed the squat, he lived in bed-and-breakfast hotels; when the April change in social security made that impossible, he moved to the "bull ring" – the walkways under Waterloo Bridge roundabout where 50 people or more sleep.

He says he gets £16 a fortnight from the Department of Social Security, and the last three days' begging has brought him £11. "The problem with work is there's a job for every 10 men and if you're homeless they don't want to know."

Half way across the bridge stands David Tripp, aged 43, tunelessly playing a mouth organ. He has spent half his life in mental hospitals and prison and now lives in a supported housing scheme in Lewisham.

He has £32 a week left after rent and says he begs to pass the time.

Twenty yards further on stands Stephen, whose ingeniously self-made coat and plastic shoes deserve a place in the Tate Gallery. He is a cheerful, grimy 37- year-old Rhodesian who swigs from a beer can.

He gets £33 a week social security, sleeps in Bedford Square or Russell Square, and reckons to make £5 from a good day's begging. "I used to line up to work at Claridge's, in the kitchens, but there are too many in the queue now. Besides, I'm rich now – I've got a radio."

THE GUARDIAN, NOVEMBER 12, 1988

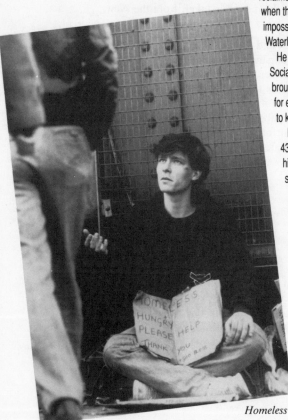

Homeless

Talk

In pairs, discuss:

● What causes people to be homeless in Britain today? List as many reasons as you can think of.
● What are the main problems facing someone who is homeless in a city? Refer to the article you have just read. What differences would there be if you were without a home in the country?
● What do Barry, David, Stephen and Njoroge have in common? In what ways are their situations different?

Assignment

Write a short story exploring the issue of homelessness. Write it from the point of view of someone who is homeless, in Britain, Kenya or anywhere else in the world.

The view from the hill

Mrs Hill kept quiet. The circumstances of Njoroge's death worried her.

Talk

In groups, make a list of the white settlers in the story. Explain the ways in which Mrs Hill's attitude to the natives was different from those of her friends.

On the following day it was all in the papers

Assignment

Write a newspaper article about the events of this story.

Stage 1   Make up a suitable headline for a newspaper with a white editor.

Stage 2   Make notes on the events of the story and on the elements of the background that you would consider relevant. You will have to expand considerably on the details given in the story.

Stage 3   Imagine that you interview Mrs Hill about what happened on the following day. Decide how many of her doubts you would present and how you would describe Mrs Hill's past treatment of natives.

Stage 4   Produce a detailed feature article on the events surrounding Njoroge's death.

Customers

Penelope Lively

Major Anglesey and Mrs Yardley-Peters worked slowly up and down the aisles of the chain store. They picked up garments and held them against each other. Mrs Yardley-Peters undid her coat, and Major Anglesey tried blouses around the broad slope of her bosom, measuring them carefully armpit to armpit. Mrs Yardley-Peters pondered over a red paisley dressing-gown, chest forty, looking from the pattern to the Major's rather ruddy complexion and gingery toothbrush moustache. Rejecting the blouses and the dressing-gown, they paused at the hosiery counter, where Mrs Yardley-Peters selected three pairs of tights (Brown Haze, Large) and paid for them at the nearest cash desk. They hesitated for a long while over ladies' v-neck lambswool sweaters, eventually deciding on a light grey size sixteen which Mrs Yardley-Peters popped into her shopping bag.

At Men's Accessories, Major Anglesey held various ties under his chin and decided on a red and navy stripe, which he folded tidily and put in his pocket. From there they wandered to the shoe section. Major Anglesey tried on a pair of brown brogues, took a step or two and shook his head, returning them to the rack. Mrs Yardley-Peters, meanwhile, had put on some black pumps – size four since, although a stout woman and not short, she had surprisingly small feet. The Major nodded approval and Mrs Yardley-Peters slipped her own shoes into the shopping bag, keeping on the pumps. Major Anglesey, at this point, glanced at his watch, said something, and the two of them moved rather more quickly to the food department where they filled a wire basket with a carton of coleslaw, two portions of cooked chicken, a packet of jam fancies and a jar of powdered coffee, lining up with those at the checkout.

The store detective, having joined them at the time of the red and navy striped tie, stood discreetly to one side. She was an unexceptional-looking woman, wearing a brown crimplene dress and fawn anorak, with a basket over one arm. The basket held, today, a bunch of bananas and a packet of Kleenex. She tended to vary the contents; meat, of course, would not do, being inclined to go bad in the heat of the store, over a long day.

Major Anglesey and Mrs Yardley-Peters passed through the checkout and back into the main part of the shop. At the entrance, they stopped for a moment, Mrs Yardley-Peters being evidently fussed in case she had lost her gloves; a search of her handbag, however, apparently put things right, and they proceeded under the blast of tropical wind issuing from somewhere in the ceiling and out into the street.

The store detective caught up with them at the zebra crossing, as they stood waiting for a lull in the traffic. She asked if they would please come back to the manager's office. The Major and Mrs Yardley-Peters received this request with considerable surprise but made no objection, except that the Major looked again at his watch and said he hoped it wouldn't take too long, as it was getting on for lunch-time.

Several sales assistants, watching the detective walk through the store a step or two behind Major Anglesey and Mrs Yardley-Peters, exchanged glances and grinned. One girl stuck her chest out and mimicked the store detective's slightly military gait; it was a standing joke that Madge, having made a capture, went all official. At that point, the crimplene dress and the anorak took on, if you knew what you were looking at, the authority of the uniform she would herself have much preferred and that she had so regretted when giving up the traffic-warden job. In most other respects, of course, her present position was far preferable. Her friends occasionally said that they didn't know how she could do a job like that, going on to add, uncertainly, that of course they supposed someone had to. . .Personally, she never found it a problem; people could be a lot more unpleasant when you handed them a parking ticket. Aggressive. Your average shop-lifter tended to crumple; she'd hardly ever – bar a gang of French schoolchildren once – had any trouble. And it was a sight warmer, on a winter afternoon, than patrolling the windy lengths of the High Street.

The manager, seated behind his desk, listened in silence to the store detective's account of the events of the last half hour. So, at first, did Mrs Yardley-Peters and Major Anglesey, until the Major began to shake his head, more in sorrow than distress, it seemed, and Mrs Yardley-Peters exclaimed, 'Oh, gracious me, no,' and then, 'No, no, it wasn't like that at all, you see we. . .' The store detective continued her account, as unemphasized as recitative.

The manager said to Mrs Yardley-Peters, 'Would you open your shopping-bag, please?'

At first Mrs Yardley-Peters did not appear to take this in. She was rummaging again in her handbag. After a moment she said, 'Ah, *there* it is.' And then, 'Oh no, I'd rather not, really, you see I've got it all sorted out, with the squashy things on top.'

The manager turned to Major Anglesey. 'It would really be much better if your wife. . .'

The Major made a small gesture. 'The lady,' he said with dignity, 'is my mistress.'

Mrs Yardley-Peters patted her hair, which was greying and set in neat ridges, a style that somehow disturbed the manager – it reminded him of something and he could not think what. 'That's right. Until my divorce comes through, you understand. Which should be before Christmas all being well but you know what lawyers are. They drag their feet so. Have you ever had dealings with lawyers, Mr er. . .?'

The manager swallowed. The store detective, who was standing beside the desk as though at attention, shifted position and drew in breath with a little hiss.

Mrs Yardley-Peters glanced round the room and located a chair. 'I must sit down for a minute. I've got this trouble with swollen ankles, and in any case. . .' – She looked down at the black pumps, frowning – 'You know, I've a horrid feeling I should have had a half size larger. These are pinching.'

The manager said, 'Can you show me a receipt for those shoes, madam?'

'Receipt?' Mrs Yardley-Peters appeared bewildered. 'Oh, from the place where you pay. . .Well, no, in fact I don't remember. . .I expect the Major paid, did you, dear? But you know I think I'll have to change them.' She turned to the store detective. 'Do you do half sizes – I didn't notice. A four-and-a-half, it would need to be.'

The manager remembered suddenly that Mrs Yardley-Peters' hairstyle reminded him of the actress who played the Duchess of Windsor in that TV series, though of course she was dark and much younger. This small satisfaction went some way to halt his mounting sense of disorientation. He said, 'I must ask you again to open your shopping-bag, madam.'

'Oh, I say' said Major Anglesey.

Mrs Yardley-Peters looked at the manager in bewilderment. 'I do think. . .' she began, and then, 'Oh well, I suppose if I'm careful.' She lifted out the packaged jam fancies and the chicken pieces. The store detective swayed forward, peering into the bag; 'That's the sweater, and that's her own shoes.'

'That's right,' said Mrs Yardley-Peters. 'You know, I wonder if I won't put them back on.' She was stacking things on the manager's desk.

The store detective straightened. She had gone quite red in the face. Her stomach rumbled.

The manager turned to Major Anglesey. 'May I please see the tie that you put in your pocket.'

The Major blinked. 'Tie? Oh, yes – rather.' He took out the tie and laid it on the desk.

'I'm not sure about that red, after all,' said Mrs Yardley-Peters. The store detective's stomach rumbled again. Mrs Yardley-Peters opened her handbag. 'I should have a magnesia tablet somewhere. Yes, here we are.' The store detective took a step backwards, violently, and landed against the wall of the office, as though at bay. 'No?' said Mrs Yardley-Peters, 'I always find they do the trick. It's getting near your lunch-time, I expect.' She eased off the black shoes, grimacing.

The manager realised he was losing his grip; tears he could cope with, protestations of innocence, truculence. He said, 'You understand that unless you can provide some proof that you paid for these goods I shall have to call the police?'

'Oh, I say,' said Major Anglesey again. Mrs Yardley-Peters, now in stockinged feet, flexed her toes; 'Oh, my goodness, I shouldn't do that, specially since it's all a silly mistake. You get into the most frightfully deep waters once you're involved with the police. My husband and I – my ex-husband, that is, all but – had an awful business once after we were the only people who saw this road accident. Witnesses, you see. Oh no – I don't think you should involve the police, not that they can't be awfully efficient sometimes, I will say that.'

The manager lined up the papers on his desk, for something to occupy his hands, and looked steadily at Major Anglesey; it was better, he found, though better wasn't really the word under the circumstances, if he simply tried to pretend the woman wasn't there. The store detective made a strangled noise. The manager said, rather sharply, 'Yes, all *right*, Mrs Hebden. Now, sir, did you pay for that tie, and did your – did the lady pay for the sweater and the shoes?'

'Oh, I don't think so,' said Major Anglesey. 'No, I don't think she would have. You see, it was a question of whether she'd left her cheque book in the car or whether. . .'

'I've got it, Rupert,' said Mrs Yardley-Peters. 'It's quite all right – it was in my bag all along, isn't that silly.'

The Major patted her shoulder. 'But at the time there was this bother about whether it was lost or not, so if anyone paid it would have been me. No doubt about that.'

'He didn't,' said the store detective.

'Really?' said Major Anglesey. 'Well, that's an extraordinary thing.' He looked at the tie. 'One wouldn't have bothered with a cheque for that, of course, it can't have cost more than a pound or two.'

'You should have had the blue one,' said Mrs Yardley-Peters. 'That's not going to be any good with your dark suit, you know.'

The manager made a compulsive movement and shot a black plastic pen container onto the floor. Major Anglesey, with cries of concern, got down and scrabbled for the pens – 'Here we are, all intact, I think.'

'So silly,' said Mrs Yardley-Peters, 'about the cheque book. Shall I pay you back while it's in my head, Rupert. I'll write *you* a cheque.'

'Look,' said the manager, with a sort of gasp, 'I simply want to. . .'

'Consider them a present my dear,' said the Major gallantly.

'You didn't pay for them,' said the store detective. The words came out as a hoarse cry and both the Major and Mrs Yardley-Peters turned to look at her in surprise. Mrs Yardley-Peters shook her head and frowned, evidently put out, 'No, no, that's absurd. You've just heard the Major say they're to be counted as a present and that's sweet of you, Rupert, though I do think we ought to keep our finances separate at least for the time being. You know, I'm wondering if the shoes may not be all right once one's worn them in a bit. Do you usually reckon,' she went on, addressing the store detective, 'on them giving a bit as you wear them?'

'Mrs Hebden is not a member of the sales staff,' said the manager. 'And in any case it is hardly a question of. . .'

The Major interrupted. 'I remember now, it all comes back – that tie was one pound ninety-five. I thought at the time good grief in real money that's all of two quid and I've got ties in my cupboard I paid four-and-six for, in the old days. Two quid for a tie, I ask you! Not,' he went on quickly, 'that it's not good value for nowadays.'

The manager rose. His collar clung to his neck and sweat trickled down inside his shirt. He went to the window and opened it.

'Yes, I was feeling it was a wee bit stuffy too,' said Mrs Yardley-Peters. 'You'd think they'd give you a bigger office, wouldn't you? But I suppose you're out and about quite a lot, looking after the shop. I always say, the thing about this sort of place is, you can see exactly what you're getting, and there's never a bit of argument about changing anything.'

Once, the manager had had to deal with an Arab lady and her three daughters, not a word of English between them, all weeping, and twenty-eight pairs of bikini briefs stuffed inside their coats. At this moment, he looked back on that occasion almost with nostalgia. He sat down again and addressed the Major. 'Now, sir, if there is any explanation you feel you'd like to give, naturally I. . .'

The note of hysteria in his voice did not escape Mrs Yardley-Peters. She said kindly, 'You know you look to me a bit under the weather, I should think you might be coming down with something. If I were you I'd. . .'

The Major tapped her reprovingly. 'Mona, I'm sure our friend here's well able to take care of himself. All he wants is to get this bit of bother sorted out so we can all be off for our dins.'

Madge Hebden, all her life, had had strong feelings about legality. She'd never, herself, stepped out of line, not once. And she believed in plain speaking. At this point she exploded.

'It's theft, that's what it is! Honest to goodness theft. Thieves! Bit of bother, indeed! I saw them with my own eyes and in all the ten months I've been in the store I've never. . .'

The manager got to his feet in one violent movement. His hands, as though acting independently of the rest of him, twitched about the surface of the desk, apparently seeking a hold on something. 'Thank you, Mrs Hebden, you've done a grand job. In this case I feel though that there may be extenuating circumstances to be taken into consideration' – he was gabbling now, looking through and beyond rather than at Major Anglesey and Mrs Yardley-Peters – 'and naturally one prefers rather than perpetrate possibly an injustice to exercise in some cases and I believe this to be one such discretion as is at one's disposal our policy in such instances being always to. . .'

'Oh dear,' said Mrs Yardley-Peters, 'I'm afraid I'm not following this very well. Could you begin again.'

The manager wiped his forehead. He said, 'Go away.'

'Eh?' said the Major.

'Please go. Just go.'

Mrs Yardley-Peters stared at him. 'Well, I must say. I think that's a bit abrupt. After all, you invited us in here, it wasn't us who wanted to come. Very well, then.' She bent down and put her shoes on. The manager, leaning across the desk, pushed towards her the contents of the shopping bag. Mrs Yardley-Peters put them carefully into it, slowly, removing things once or twice to re-arrange them. As she picked up the shoes, the lambswool sweater and the tie the store detective gave a kind of croak; the manager was silent, nerves twitching all over one side of his face.

'There,' said Mrs Yardley-Peters. She rose. 'Have you got the car-keys, Rupert, or have I?' At the door she paused and looked back. 'You know one doesn't like to interfere but I do have the most distinct impression that they overwork you people, the powers that be. You both look done in.'

Major Anglesey and Mrs Yardley-Peters walked slowly through the shop. Mid-way they paused and Major Anglesey took over the shopping bag. They stopped once to cast an eye over the shirt counter but evidently decided against any further acquisitions. At the entrance Major Anglesey held the door open for a woman with a push-chair and was then trapped for a couple of minutes by his own solicitude, as a procession of people entered from the street; at last he was able to join Mrs Yardley-Peters outside and the two of them moved away towards the multi-storey car park.

Major Anglesey drove. Mrs Yardley-Peters remarked that that poor man had seemed awfully neurotic, and the assistant rather bad-tempered. Detective, Mona, corrected the Major, they call them detective. Whatever they are, said Mrs Yardley-Peters, anyway, it's not a job I'd care for. The Major agreed. They recalled one or two previous experiences. When they reached the bungalow the Major put the car in the garage and carried the shopping bag inside. Mrs Yardley-Peters, humming to herself, removed the food items; the Major took the bag into the spare bedroom. He put the lambswool sweater, still in its plastic wrapping, into a big cupboard whose shelves were filled with many other sweaters, cardigans, shirts and pyjamas, also still in their wrappings. The tie he added to a rail already piled with ties, in a wardrobe pressed tight with suits and coats and ladies' dresses, from which dangled price tickets and labels giving washing instructions. Mrs Yardley-Peters came in and said playfully, 'Have I been a clever girl?'; the Major, without speaking, patted her bottom. 'Din-dins,' said Mrs Yardley-Peters, and the Major followed her through into the sitting-room, where the chicken pieces and the coleslaw were set out on Beatrix Potter plates. 'My turn for Jemima Puddleduck,' said Mrs Yardley-Peters. The Major poured light ale from a can into glasses decorated with cartoon mice; 'Cheers.' Mrs Yardley-Peters looked at him roguishly over the top of her glass. 'Cheers, Rupie. We've been naughty again, haven't we!' The Major, in reply, waggled his moustache, an accomplishment which had been one of his initial attractions.

A duel of words

The manager realised he was losing his grip; tears he could cope with, protestations of innocence, truculence.

In *Customers* the store detective and the manager find themselves unable to use their normal authority on this particular pair of suspected shoplifters.

Talk

Study this cartoon version of the story carefully and then, in groups, fill in what you think the characters are thinking in all the empty thought-bubbles.

In pairs, discuss which lines spoken by the couple have most effect on the shop's staff. List them and explain your choices.

Customers or shoplifters?

'Please go. Just go.'

Talk

In pairs:

- Why do you think the manager in the story sends Major Anglesey and Mrs Yardley-Peters away?
- List any evidence there is that the couple are shoplifters.
- What evidence is there that the couple *could* be customers?
- What do you think the true situation is?
- How old do you think the Major and his 'mistress' are? Give your reasons.
- What kind of people do you think the two 'customers' are on the evidence of
  a) the way they speak and what they say to the manager and store detective?
  b) the way others speak to them and treat them?
- He put the lambswool sweater, still in its plastic wrapping, into a big cupboard whose shelves were filled with many other sweaters . . . also still in their wrappings.

  What explanation can you offer for this description at the end of the story?

Assignment

'Cheers, Rupie. We've been naughty again, haven't we!'

Write another episode in the life of Mrs Yardley-Peters and Major Anglesey. Imagine that the couple continue their 'naughtiness' in another store and that things go badly wrong.

Write your episode in the form of a short play.

Develop the characters of the Major and his 'mistress' further, using the kind of dialogue you think would be appropriate for them to speak.

The causes of crime

Read

This extract adapted from *Crime* by Bruce Hugman raises a few of the possible causes of criminal behaviour.

Drink and drugs

There is no doubt that some crimes are committed by people under the influence of drink and drugs. Alcohol, LSD, glue and other chemical substances can have the effect of reducing inhibitions, or provoking violence, or of leading young people to do things they wouldn't otherwise get up to.

Like parent, like child

Some people think that criminal tendencies are inherited: that there is a 'criminal type' whose genetic make-up has more influence on their behaviour than anything else.

However, there is no convincing evidence that genetic make-up determines human behaviour in this way.

We all inherit aspects of our temperament and ability to some extent, as well as our physical characteristics, but they all seem to be greatly influenced by outside factors as well.

The opportunist criminal

There are some people who may not be regular criminals, but who will take an opportunity if it is offered: if the window of a house or car is left open. . .

There's no answer

Human beings are so vastly complicated that we shall probably never understand what makes them like they are.

But there are some indications. . .

In terms of numbers the vast majority of criminals are male and 'working class' – that is they come from families with semi-skilled or unskilled workers in them, are usually wage earning, and, in general, not very senior in their jobs.

Talk

In pairs,
- Which part of this information do you find most surprising?
- How many reasons can you think of that could explain why people shoplift? List them.

The impulse to steal

Read

The most surprising people can be thieves

Pensioner in bank raid

By Martin Wainright

The Old Baily listened spellbound yesterday to the tale of a pensioner's doomed attempt to hold hostages at a London bank and rob it of £85,000. Mrs Peggy Barlow, aged 70, of West Kensington, skipped her weekly bridge party to carry out the raid, travelling on her bus pass and armed with a perfume spray which she pretended was a gun.

She grabbed a customer at the bank and bundled her into the manager's office, pressing the perfume canister into her side in a style she had noticed on a TV film about Chicago gangsters. Then she ordered everyone to keep quiet and demanded all the money in the bank, modifying this to £85,000 after a delay which led to her shout: "Hurry up, I'm desperate!"

Mrs Barlow, who walks with the help of a stick and is a bank manager's widow herself, admitted demanding the money with menaces from Mr David Ball, manager of the National Westminster Bank in Kensington High Street.

Her counsel, Mr Brian Barker, said that the story was almost beyond belief and involved an "extraordinary aberration" brought on by threats of bankruptcy. Mrs Barlow who has two grown-up children, had debts of £70,000 and faced daily demands from creditors in the weeks before her raid.

"A younger person may have been able to take this desperate financial situation in their stride, but it worried this lady so much that she turned bandit," said Mr Barker.

The court heard that Mrs Barlow had put herself in some danger, with armed police wearing bullet-proof jackets sent to the bank after staff pressed a panic button. Although her planning was sophisticated she reckoned without her hostage, Mrs Julien Watkins.

Mr Peter Doyle, prosecuting, said that Mrs Watkins had suddenly decided to have a go and had pinned Mrs Barlow to the wall with the help of the bank manager. Three policemen arrived and arrested Mrs Barlow.

The Recorder of London, Sir James Miskin QC, said that the raid had been doomed from the start but had still led to a lot of trouble. He added that before the offence Mrs Barlow had led a 'socially splendid and responsible' life and had been too proud to ask for help with her finances (which have since been resolved by the sale of her cottage). Sentencing her to nine months' imprisonment, suspended for a year, he warned her not to do anything idiotic again.

Mrs Barlow thanked him and left the court to have a glass of Scotch and describe how she had planned a 'kind and gentle' raid in contrast to the ones she saw on television

"I must have had a brainstorm. I'm normally a very placid and timid person," she said. "Mercifully, everyone has been very kind and understanding and I've promised not to break the law again."

THE GUARDIAN OCTOBER 6, 1984

Talk

There are several unanswered questions in this unusual report. For example, if Mrs Barlow was short of money, why didn't she sell her cottage earlier instead of trying to steal money from a bank? Talk about these possible interpretations of the events leading up to the bank raid:

- Mrs Barlow had always been hopeless with money and ran up terrible debts after her husband's death.
- Mrs Barlow had gone on a spending spree to overcome her unhappiness after the death of her husband.
- Mrs Barlow was a compulsive gambler.
- Mrs Barlow had been a criminal all her life, but had never before been caught.
- Mrs Barlow had fallen into debt because of her alcoholism.
- Mrs Barlow was a confused old woman who was so worried about her money problems that she planned the bankraid.
- Mrs Barlow hoped that the raid would fail and that she would then get someone to help her.

Which of these explanations do you think are closest to the truth? What is *your* explanation of Mrs Barlow's situation?

Assignment

Write a newspaper article, similar to the one you have just read, but based on the events of *Customers*.

Imagine that the story had ended differently, with the Major and Mrs Yardley-Peters being charged, arrested by the police and taken to court.

A Manager's point of view

Read

In this interview a manager of a large store answers questions about the ways in which the store deals with shoplifters.

What kind of people make up the bulk of the shoplifters you deal with?
There are really two main groups, young people in the 16 to 20 age range and the elderly.

The elderly?
Yes surprisingly we spend a lot of our time dealing with elderly people. Some are confused and several are just plain forgetful. We get some who have seen something on television which they can't afford. So they come to a store like ours and take it. Occasionally we find that they are just bored or sometimes very unhappy. I suppose being caught by us gets them some attention.

Could you outline the procedures that you would use if you suspected someone of shoplifting?
The first thing is that the store detective would catch the person, normally just as he or she is leaving the shop. There is then a set form of words that have to be used. At this stage the person is taken to the manager, to a small bare room a bit like the one we're in! I would ask the store detective to give a factual account of what had been observed and tell the suspect not to say anything until this part

is finished. We then search the suspect's bag and coat. Most people give up at this stage and we then call the police.

Would this be the same for all types of suspect?
No. We try and stop old people before they have left the store, as nine times out of ten they are just being forgetful and this saves embarrassment. For youngsters we sometimes agree with the police that they will be fetched from the police station by their parents after a caution. Again for most this works very well. They've just been larking about and find the experience of being in a cell even for a few hours quite enough to teach them a lesson.

Can you tell me what kind of things store detectives look out for?
As you can appreciate this is quite sensitive information. But I can tell you that people with large bags or large coats, especially on warm days, certainly arouse our suspicions. Most detectives get an instinct for browsers who aren't really browsing.

Do you record what is happening in cases like the ones you have been describing?
Yes. We use a standard form in which the store detective has to act as a witness to precisely what has happened and when.

How much are you affected by the way people dress and speak?
I'd like to say not at all, but in all honesty you do find yourself being influenced. Obviously we're not going to take much notice of someone who is drunk, and well-spoken people do tend to make a better impression. They tend to get angry and start threatening things. They're not always what they seem though. I remember one very well-dressed couple of ladies. Wearing fur coats and carrying expensive bags. They kept shouting and protesting until the moment that I pulled a five pack of expensive lingerie out of one of their bags!

Do you have any other particular memories?
There was one woman who tried to fool us with the single receipt trick.

How does that work?
Well, we caught her with a bottle of Asti Spumante which we were sure she had taken. As soon as we took her up here, she brought out a receipt for a bottle just like it. However, and you might like to tell your students this, she hadn't bargained on our new tills. They tell you exactly when it was bought and from which till. So we got her that way! In her bags were two cameras, two joints of beef, two shirts and for each one there was only one receipt.

How much theft is there from a store like yours?

We estimate that about one per cent of all our stock is stolen or not accounted for in some other way. It's a lot really, but we are getting much better at catching thieves.

Talk

- In what ways does the manager suggest that the store deals particularly sympathetically with elderly people?
- What information does the manager give that relates to *Customers*? Make a list.
- How do you think the couple in the story would have got on with the manager in this interview? Explain your answers in detail.

Assignment

The manager described the process through which all suspects are put. Using a copy of the form opposite, complete the detailed report that the store detective in the story might have written.

The store detective's name should appear after the words STATEMENT OF. . . . Use information from the story and add any other appropriate details you might wish to include.

You may wish to continue on another sheet.

Statement of Witness (C.J. Act, 1967, S.9; M.C. Act, 1980, S. 102; M.C. Rules, 1981, r. 70)

STATEMENT OF..

Age of Witness (date of birth)..

Occupation of Witness...

Address and Telephone Number..

....

....

This statement, (consisting of .... pages each signed by me*), is true to the best of my knowledge and belief and I make it knowing that, if it is tendered in evidence, I shall be liable to prosecution if I have willfully stated in it anything which I know to be false or do not believe to be true.

Dated the .... day of .... 19 ....

Signed ....Signature witnessed by.......................................

....

....

....

....

....

....

....

....

....

....

....

....

....

....

....

....

....

....

Signed ....Signature witnessed by.......................................

*Delete if not applicable

No. 991

(Print name...)

Page No. [   ]

Additional assignments

These assignments are each based on more than one story. They might well be suitable for longer studies required by some GCSE examinations or for more independent research.

Assignment 1

Education for change

In *Getting Sent For, Prize Giving, Bright Thursdays* and *The Stolen Party* the power of education is evident in very different ways. Describe the different pictures presented of education in three stories. In what ways are the lessons learned at school as powerful as those learned at home?

How can schools attempt to provide equal opportunities for people of all cultures and all classes?

Describe how such a school might work – what subjects it would offer, what rules it would have and how it would treat its parents.

Assignment 2

Officials and 'customers' – the headmistress and the manager

People are often treated very differently depending on their 'class' or appearance. Describe Mrs Sharp as you think she must have appeared to the headmistress. Describe the two customers as they would have appeared to the manager of the shop.

What conclusions do you draw from these descriptions?

Write a short scene in which the customers are 'reversed', the Major and Mrs Yardley-Peters appearing in the headmistress's office **or** Mrs Sharp being accused of shoplifting.

Assignment 3

The children's point of view – Siobhan – Laura – Rosaura

Imagine what would hapen if these three children were to meet up in later life at a party, at a conference, on a course or wherever you choose.

Write a short play in which they start to talk about their different upbringings and remember important moments from them. Try to bring out clearly each character's different point of view.

Assignment 4

Growing up

Which story presents the family situation that is closest to your own? Describe it fully, making it clear in what ways it is similar to your own.

Which 'parent' in this collection would you most like to have? Explain your choice carefully and fully.

What are the qualities you most look for in people who are responsible for bringing up children, whether at school or at home?

Assignment 5

Interview a range of people about their memories of school, home and teenage life. Focus particularly on some of the issues of class raised in these stories. Write a feature about some of the people you interview that would be suitable for a local newspaper.

Assignment 6

Write a short story in which characters from at least three different stories appear.

Assignment 7

Write a review for a class journal or newspaper of the two stories that you enjoyed most in this anthology. Comment on what happens (without telling the ending), characters, what you liked about the writer's style or message and anything else you found interesting.

Acknowledgements

The authors would like to thank Elaine and Rosie for their support and encouragement.

The authors and publishers wish to thank the following who have kindly given permission for the use of copyright material:

Basil Blackwell Ltd for material from *Hooligans or Rebels?* by Stephen Humphries, 1981; Jonathan Cape Ltd for 'Getting Sent For' by Agnes Owens from *Lean Tales* by Alasdair Gray, Agnes Owens and James Kelman, 1985; Stephen Cook for 'Growing army of beggars in London', *The Guardian*, 12 November 1988; Michael Durham for material from *The Guardian*, 20 December 1988; Alan Gilbey for 'Disruptive Minority'; Victor Gollancz Ltd for material from *How it Feels to be Adopted* by Jill Krementz, 1984; William Heinemann Ltd for 'Customers' from *Corruption* by Penelope Lively, 1984; Heinemann Educational Books Ltd for material from *Secret Lives* by Ngugi wa Thiongo; Longman Group Ltd for 'Bright Thursdays' by Olive Senior from *Summer Lightening*, Longman Caribbean, 1986; Macmillan Publishers Ltd for an extract from *Passbook No. F. 47927* by M. Likimani, 1985; Monthly Review Foundation for material from *Mau Mau Within* by Donald Barnett and Karari Njama, 1970 (Copyright © 1970 by Donald Barnett and Karari Njama); *The Observer* for 'Minding Your Manners', 4 September 1988; Pan Books Ltd for 'The Stolen Party' by Liliana Heker from *Other Fires* by Alberto Manguel; Sheba Feminist Publishers for 'Prize Giving' from *Water's Edge* by Moy McCrory, 1985; Unwin Hyman Ltd for material from *Memories of Kenya*, ed. Arnold Curtis, 1986; Martin Wainwright for 'Pensioner in bank raid', *The Guardian*, 6 October 1984.

The authors and publishers would like to acknowledge the following photographic sources:

Barnaby's Picture Library page 52; Mary Evans Picture Library page 59; Mansell Collection page 13; Popperfoto pages 26, 60, 72, 78; Topham Picture Library pages 73, 75, 83.

The publishers have made every effort to trace the copyright holders, but if they have inadvertently overlooked any, they will be pleased to make the necessary arrangements at the first opportunity.

Illustrations by Taurus Graphics
Cartoon by Brian Walker